CRYSTAL UPRISING
THE AWAKENING

CRYSTAL UPRISING
THE AWAKENING

ADDIE ANTHONY

iUniverse LLC
Bloomington

CRYSTAL UPRISING
The Awakening

This is a work of fiction. All of the characters, names, incidents,
organizations, and dialogue in this novel are either the products
of the author's imagination or are used fictitiously.

iUniverse books may be ordered through booksellers or by contacting:

iUniverse LLC
1663 Liberty Drive
Bloomington, IN 47403
www.iuniverse.com
1-800-Authors (1-800-288-4677)

Because of the dynamic nature of the Internet, any web addresses or
links contained in this book may have changed since publication and
may no longer be valid. The views expressed in this work are solely those
of the author and do not necessarily reflect the views of the publisher,
and the publisher hereby disclaims any responsibility for them.

Any people depicted in stock imagery provided by Thinkstock are models,
and such images are being used for illustrative purposes only.
Certain stock imagery © Thinkstock.

ISBN: 978-1-4917-3125-3 (sc)
ISBN: 978-1-4917-3126-0 (e)

Library of Congress Control Number: 2014906834

Printed in the United States of America.

iUniverse rev. date: 04/17/2014

To my family, the most important people who are part of my life.
Thank you for always telling me to at no time give up on love.

To everyone who is still searching for that special someone, never
give up. Don't go searching for love. It will always find you.

PREFACE

This book came to me in a glance of a daydream. I saw myself in a situation of never really knowing what the word *love* really meant. I didn't know the difference between lust or arising affection of the heart. In that very second, I told myself not to be afraid anymore and that the only way to overcome my fears was to write down what kind of love I always desired.

So now I write this story from my mind and let the world imagine my meaning for love through these characters' eyes. I can only hope that this version of love will open readers' hearts and minds to others.

PROLOGUE

I could feel the tension in their bodies. With every step, their feet firmly pressed into the earth. The fast pace of their heartbeats echoed on the outside of their chests. The vibration from the air moving from their lungs to the outside of their bodies was very quick and sharp. They moved quickly through the woods.

"Faster," I could hear the mysterious woman yell to her companion, which, to me, sounded like a whisper within my ear.

Suddenly, out of the darkness of the woods appeared a man, stopping them right in their paths. Frozen in fear, they both stared deeply into the tall but slim man's eyes. Wearing a very nice suit, he stood there in front of them. His skin shone from the moonlight, which made it very difficult to focus in on his face, but his voice was very strong and dominant. Before they could say a word, he lifted both arms to grab their necks very quickly and firmly. And within a second, they were lifted from the ground into the air. It was if there were never anyone there.

Am I next? Will I to be taken away?

CHAPTER 1

Out of nowhere, a hand grabbed my shoulder. Gasping for air, I opened my eyes, sat up in my bed, and looked around my room. Realizing it was just a dream, I moved my dark brown hair from my face. I could feel the sweat moving down my entire caramel, slim but athletic body. I turned my head to the right to look at my alarm clock on my nightstand.

"Six fifteen. Damn, I'm going to be late."

Forcing myself to move, I got out of bed and rushed to my bathroom to take a shower. While showering, I couldn't help but think about my dream, the pain I felt for the two of them, and the look in their eyes as they stood frozen in place by fear.

What did it mean? Most importantly, how in any way does it relate to me? Turning off the water in the shower, I reached out and grabbed my towel from the rack against the wall. I wrapped the towel around me while stepping out of the shower. Drying off, I began to get dressed for school. Walking over to my bed, I looked down at the outfit I had chosen the night before to wear, a simple white lace-back tank, a pair of light jeans with tan outlining, and tan biker babe booties.

Simple, I know, but still very fashionable, I thought to myself while getting dressed. Walking over to my mirror, I stood there and thought to myself, *Wow, today will be my first day as a senior.* Standing there, I thought back at the primary three years of my high school career. It made me realize just how fast they flew by. And now, I was a senior in high school. They say you should have a plan for your future by this time and you should know what college you are going to attend or even if you just wanted to go backpacking somewhere overseas. I should have had something in mind of what I wanted to do with my future; nevertheless, I was nowhere near being close. I had thought into the future a lot, sometimes more than twice a day. I never saw myself as a briefcase kind of girl or even backpacking for that matter. Possibly, this year was the one for me. Perhaps I would have it all figured out. Or I hoped.

Looking away from my mirror, I grabbed my bag, car keys, and cell phone off my desk in my room. Refocusing myself back into my mirror, I took one more look at myself and took a deep breath. "You're going to be fine," I told myself.

I headed downstairs. As I reached the bottom of the stairs and rounded the corner, I could hear my aunt Kristen and uncle Matthew's sweet laughter coming from the kitchen. *Those two really make sure I have my most important meal of the day.*

I couldn't ask for a more perfect aunt and uncle. Kristen was a second grade teacher. She was a little on the short side, but she had the brightest smile that just lit up a room. Matthew was a local pediatrician at the hospital farther in town. He might look tough and built strong on the outside, but on the inside, he was as soft as a new teddy bear for a newborn baby. Matthew and Kristen were like my parents. They both told me that my mom and dad had died in a car accident when I was just a baby, and they took me in and raised me as their own here in Jackson Pete, North Carolina. Sad, I know, but I was grateful for them every day. *They are both flawless in their own way*, I thought to myself.

I walked up to the counter and sat down on the stool.

My aunt placed my plate in front of me and smiled. "Good morning, Nichole." Her voice was as calm as the river water flowing down a bank.

"Good morning," I said through a smile.

My uncle walked behind me and placed a kiss on the top of my head. I just knew he could smell my lavender hair shampoo scent in my hair.

"How did you sleep?" Uncle Matthew asked.

I sat there in silence for a few seconds before I answered his question, knowing I shouldn't lie and should tell the truth about my dream. I gazed up and saw the two of them staring in each other's eyes and sharing a kiss. In that moment, it was pure happiness. I couldn't ruin that. So I smiled slightly back at him.

"Yeah, I slept great." I quickly shifted my attention onto my plate of wheat toast with fresh fruit salad.

"So are you excited about school today?" Kristen asked. "You're a senior in high school." She sounded more excited than I was.

"Yeah, I hope to get the title of cheer captain this year, so all is looking well." The buzzing from my phone caught my attention.

Grabbing my phone off of the counter, I read the text from Amy: "Can I have a ride to school?"

"Sure. On my way. Be there in fifteen," I replied back.

"I have to leave early to pick up Amy. She needs a ride to school." I took a drink of my orange juice and got up from my seat. Grabbing my things, I rushed up to the both of them. "Bye! I love you guys. Thanks for breakfast." I gave them both a kiss on the cheek.

I headed out the door, and as the door closed behind me, I could hear Kristen's voice yell to me, "Have a great day!"

I would have turned around to tell her thanks, but I was already running late. Plus, I had to pick up Amy.

"I can't believe she will turn eighteen years old tomorrow. They grow up so fast," said Kristen.

"Yes, but don't worry. We raised a smart kid." Matthew walked behind her and kissed her on the cheek.

"Yes, we did." She smiled.

CHAPTER 2

On the road driving to Amy's house, I could not stop thinking about my aunt and uncle from this morning. The way they were looking at each other, it was like nothing else in the world mattered. It was so breathtaking to me. I hoped that I would be as lucky as they were one day.

To find a love that was as pure and strongly desired as they had would truly be a blessing. I was in a relationship with a guy named Tyler, but nothing—no heat, no passion, no nothing—was there. He was such a nice guy. Even though he was my first official boyfriend, to me, it felt more of a huge crush that was getting old. *I don't want to hurt him. I want more than just a crush. Is it really wrong of me to want more?*

Pulling in front of Amy's house, I beeped the horn to let her know that I was out front. I had known Amy for almost five years now. She was just so loyal to me, and she always did the right thing. Now even though her blonde hair and green eyes didn't match with my dark brown hair and brown eyes, we still considered each other as sisters.

"Hey, Nichole," she said in the most excited voice as she got inside the car.

"Hey, Amy," I said with the biggest smile upon my face.

"We are seniors!" Amy screamed out at the top of her lungs.

"I know," I said with the biggest sigh up under my breath.

I could feel Amy's eyes just piercing into my skin as I knew what she was about to ask me. "How could you not be excited about this, Nichole? We are finally seniors in high school. And the best part is that we will be freshmen in college after this year."

"It's not that I'm not excited. I'm just nervous about this year. Plus, when this year ends, what am I doing after high school? I have no clue as to what I want to do with my life." Keeping my focus on the road, I continued having a conversation with her while driving to school. "I'm seventeen years old, a senior in high school, and I have a boyfriend whom I am not interested in. Trust me. I know how terrible that last part sounds, but it's the truth. I'm just going to end up as a lowlife living with her aunt and uncle. How sad is that?"

There was the longest pause in the car. I had never heard or seen Amy so lost for words before. She just sat there and stared at the dashboard.

Finally, after what seemed like forever, Amy began to talk to me. "Nichole, you do not have to have everything figured out right now. Nevertheless, you do need to tell Tyler the truth," she told me with the most calmness in her voice.

Not knowing what to say back to her, I just sat there lost in thought.

"Nichole," Amy gently yelled.

"What!" I replied to her.

"You need to tell him the truth."

I then took a short sigh under my breath. "I know. I just can't hurt him, Amy."

Amy touched my shoulder with comfort. "You're hurting him by not telling him the truth. He is going around thinking everything is okay when he is really one step away from being single."

"You're right. I will tell him today."

We talked the rest of the time along the way to school. I pulled up in the school parking lot that only seniors were allowed to park in. Amy and I could see Tyler waiting for me by the tree in front of the school where we met each other every morning.

Looking at him, I couldn't help but feel terrible about myself. I really hoped that we could still be friends, no matter how long it may take.

Waiting beside him was our good friend, Chelsea. Chelsea and I had known each other for only two years. She was a blown-out diva even though her kind heart that she tried so hard to hide always overpowered her diva side. Well, in most cases, it did.

I turned off the engine and stepped out of the car. I could feel this deep feeling in the bottom of my stomach. It felt as if I were going to be sick. Although I didn't want to admit it to myself, all I was feeling was the truth to tell Tyler not wanting to come out. *How could I bring myself to tell him that I just can't be with him anymore? Yes, I care about him, but I am not in love with him.*

While walking up to Tyler, he had the cutest smile upon his face.

"Hey you." He took me by the waist and pulled me close to him.

"Hey," I replied with a small smile.

As I then tried to pull away, Tyler gently grabbed my face and kissed me on the lips. "I've missed you this summer," said Tyler with the most flirtatious tone to his voice.

"That's so sweet," I said with a short pause in between words. "Hey, do you think we could talk later?" I hoped the question itself wouldn't make him a little curious to ask about what.

He simply replied, "Sure. How about you meet me under the bleachers on the football field during first period?"

"Yeah, I'll see you there." I had a smirk of a smile on my face.

Tyler subsequently kissed me again and said to me softly, "Okay, I'll see you afterward. I love you," he told me with the most confident look into his eyes, like he was so sure about us.

However, even though he was certain about us, I wasn't. I couldn't say "I love you" back to him, especially if I didn't mean it. All I could say to him was, "Okay, I'll see you later."

He then smiled at me and walked away. I could sense the sick feeling in the bottom of my stomach slowly fade with every step that Tyler took further and further in another place from me. Pulling my hair back out of my face, I turned around to face Amy and Chelsea.

They both were looking at me like I was the biggest jerk on school grounds.

"What? Why are you two looking at me like that?"

"Wow." Chelsea rolled her eyes at me.

"What?" I repeated.

"He just told you that he loved you, and you didn't even say it back."

Fixing my bag on my shoulder, I couldn't think of any words to come out of my mouth. I just stood there feeling so guilty. Then finally words began stumbling out of my mouth. "No, I just . . . Look, guys, I know, okay? That's why I'm breaking up with him today."

Even though the words came out, I still didn't think I would have the courage to break up with Tyler. Even though I knew in my heart that it would be hard, it was the right thing to do.

"Can we please just head to class?" I said in a very sad tone.

Walking up to the open school doors, I felt Chelsea's arm come around my shoulder.

"Are you going to be okay?" she asked.

"Yeah." I gently smiled.

I just wanted to go to class and get the day over with. Walking through the doors to the school, a very good friend crossed my mind.

"I wonder where Kyle is." I smiled. "I haven't seen him all summer. We both have been really busy."

"Are you serious, Nichole?" asked Amy with a very annoyed tone to her voice.

"You know I will never understand why you are friends with that guy. I know he is so weird," said Chelsea.

"Okay, first of all, I have known him longer than both of you." I turned to face them. "And he's one of my best friends, so give him some slack, please."

Walking into the school hallway, they both agreed and apologized. Turning around, I looked down the hallway and saw Kyle getting a book out of his locker.

"Hey, I'll be right back." I walked toward Kyle.

I missed him so much over the summer that, in a sense, I could say I missed him a little too much. I didn't know what it was about Kyle that made me feel like I was safe with him, like we were meant to be friends.

Sneaking up behind him, I gently tapped him on the shoulder. Of course when he turned around, he had to look down at me because he was like a giant compared to me.

"Hey," he said with excitement.

I reached up and gave him the biggest hug around his slim, athletic body. As I let go and pulled away, I couldn't do anything but smile at him.

"So how was your summer? I missed you," he said.

"How sweet," I replied. "I missed you too. But I can literally say that my summer was the same, you know, going to cheer camp and a couple of parties. And I also did some volunteer work at the hospital. I actually think I'm going to continue to do that. I learned a lot. What about you?" I smiled.

Turning his head away from his locker, he smiled at me. "Party girl, huh? I like it." He had a flirty smile on his face.

"Shut up." I smiled while playfully hitting him on the shoulder. "Seriously, what did you do this summer?"

He then pulled his camera out of his locker and took a picture of me. "You know, photography camp."

"So is that for your wall collection?" I smiled.

With the biggest smirk on his face, he said, "Of course. You know I love taking pictures of beautiful things."

There was a short pause between us. Then I said in a calm voice, "You know, if I didn't know any better, I would think you are flirting with me."

"Don't flatter yourself." Kyle put his camera back in his locker.

I rolled my eyes as I hit him playfully on his arm again.

Walking from his locker, Kyle asked me. "So," he said after a pause, "what are you doing for your birthday tomorrow?"

While looking a little confused, I began to answer his question. "Wow, I didn't really think about it. To tell you the truth, my aunt and uncle didn't even mention anything this morning. They must have forgotten. I don't know. I really don't want to do anything. I can't believe you remembered."

"How could I forget? We've only celebrated each other's birthdays since we were three years old."

"Well, I'm not really in a birthday mood," I said while walking.

"Why not? Everyone should celebrate her birthdays," he said.

Exhaling a single breath that felt like relief, I told him why I wasn't in a birthday mood. "I'm breaking up with Tyler today."

"Really," said Kyle with a very fake, sad expression on his face.

"Yes," I replied. "I just don't feel the same way about him anymore, and I can't keep dragging him along like everything is okay when I know it's not. I don't know. Do you think I'm doing the right thing?"

Kyle gently turned my shoulder for me to face him. "Yes. What you are doing is the right thing to do. You can't keep leading him on. Trust me. You're doing the right thing. You know I'm here for you, right?" he said to me with a sweet smile of comfort.

"Yes, I know you are always there for me."

"How can I not be? You are my best friend, Nichole."

I couldn't help but smile back at him. I honestly didn't know what it was about Kyle. He truly made me feel like everything was going to be okay.

"So," said Kyle, "how about I come over tonight? And we can eat junk food and watch movies all night."

"That sounds great." I smiled.

"All right, so I'll see you tonight?"

"Fine," I replied.

We both agreed to the plans for tonight. We hugged each other and went our separate ways to class. I turned around for a quick second to glance back at Kyle walking to his class. Turning back around, I could see Amy and Chelsea quickly glance at me from their lockers with a very muddled look on their faces. Walking up to them, I could tell this conversation was going to be interesting.

"What? Why are you guys looking at me like that?" I asked while standing in front of them.

"Kyle, really?" Amy had a very disapproving sound in her voice. "You haven't even broken up with Tyler yet, Nichole."

"You are so into Kyle," said Chelsea in the most deviant tone.

"No, I'm not," I replied.

"Yes, you are. Come on. Everyone can see it, Nichole," Chelsea said.

"We are just friends." I had a very annoyed look on my face.

Pushing herself off her locker, Chelsea said to me in a very simple voice, "If you say so."

Dropping the conversation, we all started walking to class. Walking into first period, I started to think to myself, *Could I really have feelings for Kyle? Of course I couldn't. He is my best friend. I wouldn't dare do anything to jeopardize that.*

CHAPTER 3

Taking a seat in class, I realized that I was officially a senior. I could still remember sitting in first period in Mr. Greeting's class, the way he stood in front of the classroom explaining to us that our high school years would go by so fast.

Now here I was, sitting in first period as a senior. It was a little scary to think that, in only ten months, I would be graduating from high school and I had no idea of what to do with my life. I couldn't say the same for everyone else. Chelsea would be going to New York to start an internship with a very large fashion design company. Amy would be at Yale to go to school to become a lawyer, and Kyle was going to California to pursue his photography career. *I feel so out of place. What am I meant to do with my life? Will it be something important, or will I just flat-out be a huge disappointment?*

Sitting at my desk thinking to myself, my back pocket began to vibrate. Carefully without getting caught, I took my phone out of my pocket. Looking at my phone on my desk, I saw it was Tyler, who texted me, "I'm at the bleachers. Come meet me. Hurry."

Taking a second to get the courage to raise my hand, I took a deep breath and exhaled. I raised my hand and asked to use the hall pass. Walking out of the classroom down the hallway leading me to the bleachers, I could feel the deep pain in my stomach come back. The closer I got to Tyler, the worse the feeling became.

Walking up to Tyler, I wanted so badly to turn around and run. Even so, I knew this had to be done, not later but now. Leaning into me, he gently kissed my cheek. I turned my head away, stopping his lips from touching mine.

"Are you okay?" He took a few steps back.

My eyes drifted off him and onto the ground. "Tyler," I said with a slight pause. "I can't do this anymore."

He looked at me very confused. "Do what, Nichole?"

"You and me. This. Us. I can't pretend like there is still something between us. I can't keep dragging you along thinking one thing when what I am feeling is something totally different. Trust me. It's not you. It's me. I'm the one with the problem. You are a really great guy." I took my eyes off the ground and focused on him.

Taking two steps away, he looked at me with disappointment and disbelief. "Are you seriously doing this right now? You hit me with the 'it's not you; it's me' speech. Really, Nichole?"

"I'm sorry," I said low under my breath.

He took two steps back up to me and gently took my hands into his. "Please don't do this." He pleaded with me.

Looking up at him, I could see the tears forming in his eyes. *Those tears are my fault. Nevertheless, I have to do this. It's for the best for both of us.*

I gently put his right cheek in the palm of my left hand. "I am so sorry." I slowly leaned in to kiss his lips for the last time.

Right before our lips touched, he gently grabbed my left hand and pulled it away from his face. "No, I can't, I can't do this."

He let go from my hand and turned away from me, and without even looking back, he just walked off. I felt loathsome on the inside for hurting Tyler that way. I also felt very relieved that it was officially over. Now he could genuinely be with someone who could really love him completely.

Walking back to class, I went the opposite direction of Tyler. Walking down past the football locker room was not one of my favorite halls. Nevertheless, after breaking up with Tyler, I would put up with this stinky hall over a very awkward position.

While walking down the hall, my back pocket began to vibrate again. I pulled it out to read the text. "Where are you? We're about to take a pop quiz. Amy."

Putting all my attention into my phone instead of where I was going, I suddenly bumped into someone and dropped my phone.

"Oh, man. Don't be broken." I knelt down to pick up my phone.

Then as my hand touched my phone to pick it up, another hand landed on top of mine. I looked up at eye level to see who the hand belonged to. Locking eyes with the most handsome guy I'd ever seen in my life, I could not help but notice all of his features. His eyes were hazel brown. His lips looked so soft and pink. His skin was a light tan color, a beautiful mixture of black and white. He had a short haircut. His face was perfect.

"Are you okay?" The handsome stranger stood to his feet.

I stood up slowly, never taking my eyes off him. I smiled without saying a word and shook my head yes.

"Is your phone okay?" the stranger asked.

I looked down at my phone. Realizing that my phone was okay, I smiled and shook my head yes again.

"You don't talk very much, do you?" he asked.

Still in a daze, I forced my brain to work and make me say something. Then very slowly, I said yes. "I mean I'm sorry for bumping into you. And yes, my phone is okay. I'm sorry. I should have been paying more attention."

Standing there gazing back at one another, he finally said something to break the silence. "So what brings you down this hall? You're not skipping class, are you?"

"No, I am just avoiding an awkward situation," I said to him.

"Oh, been there done that." He smiled.

Continuing to smile at him, I managed to say something. "Well, I should head back to class." A smile appeared on my face.

While walking away, I quickly turned back to get another look at him. "Wow," I said to myself. "Is it possible for someone to be that handsome? I don't know what it is about him. However, I have to get to know him. Everything about him. To me, he is a lock that must be opened."

Walking back into the classroom, the teacher handed me a pop quiz and told me to be seated. Judging by the tone in his voice, I could tell he was a little aggravated with me for taking so long to come from my bathroom break. I sat back at my desk and took my quiz. Forty-five minutes later, the school bell rang. The rest of the day went by quite quickly.

The last bell rang for the day. Chelsea, Amy, and I headed to the girls' locker room to get ready for cheer practice.

"So," Chelsea said, "who do you think cheer captain is going to be this year?"

"Nichole, for sure," Amy said right away while looking at me.

"Thanks, Amy. I hope I do, but if I don't, it's fine. I mean, as long as I'm cheering, I'm fine."

Giving a very unconvinced look, Amy closed her locker door and stared at me with disbelief. "Whatever. You know you want and deserve that title, Nichole. You are the best on the squad. Plus, you have been an All-American cheerleader every year since the ninth grade."

"Okay, you're right. I do want to be captain." I turned around with excitement to face her.

"Anyways," said Chelsea, "on a whole other topic of the day. Did you do it?"

The excitement quickly escaped my face, for I knew what she was pertaining to. "Yes, I broke up with Tyler." I rolled my eyes. I closed my locker door to face them both.

The two of them looked at me as if they felt sorry for me.

"Are you going to be okay?" Amy asked.

"Yes, now Tyler and I can both find someone who makes us really happy."

"You know what? You're right," said Chelsea. "Now, let's put on our cheerful faces and go give these guys on the field something to look at."

They both hugged me, and we headed out of the locker room to the field.

CHAPTER 4

Walking on to the football field, I could hear everyone whispering who she thought the cheer captain should be this year. The only name who continued to pop up was Samantha Givens. She was basically the town princess. Anything she wanted, it was hers. Her dad was also the town mayor so that played a huge part in it with no questions asked. In all fairness, she was decent.

Well, not as excellent as me. I mean, come on. I have over eight years of elite gymnastics training, I'm an All-American cheerleader, and I practiced in ballet and modern dance for the past ten years. Nevertheless, who's bragging?

We all sat down in front of the coach in a circle. She told us how proud she was of us last season and how she was so excited about this season coming. Standing to her feet, she began her speech that was the same, word for word, every year on who she felt was captain and cocaptain material.

"Well, ladies," she said, "last season was a challenge for us. It started off a little rough at the beginning. But at the end, we came together and conquered all of our goals. Do any of you ladies know why?"

"Teamwork!" we all shouted.

"That's right, ladies. Teamwork. However, in order for teamwork to happen, we have to have leadership. Now, I think I speak for everyone when I say that our captain and cocaptain last year are going to be very hard to follow. All last season, I was secretly watching each one of you on your skills, attitudes, grades, and all-around personality, making sure that, this year, the leadership of this team would be just as great as last year's.

"Now, after a lot of thinking, I have finally decided who your captain and cocaptain will be this year. These two females are leaders in my book, and I know you will be proud to call them your captain and cocaptain of this squad, as I am.

"First up, your cocaptain is . . ." She paused for a very short time. "Ms. Nichole Gibson."

Are you serious? All the while, I made my facial expression different from my train of thought.

"And your captain is Ms. Samantha Givens."

This is not fair at all. But of course, my face and thoughts were totally different.

"Okay, ladies, now that that is done, let's warm up with some cheer stunts."

Walking over to my group for stunts, I noticed that Kyle was in the bleachers, taking photos of me. I couldn't help but smile at him. He was such a nerd. Getting into position to go up in my stunt, I had to make sure to focus on what I was doing.

"Ready!" the coach yelled.

"One, two," the group said, counting.

Going up into my stunt was a piece of cake. While in my stunt, I glanced at Kyle. I noticed someone behind him, the handsome stranger from the hall. He was smiling at me.

Putting all of my focus on him, I then lost control of what I was doing. I became unstable and fell hard on the ground out of my stunt. It knocked the wind out of me, and I laid on the ground for a few seconds before I opened my eyes. I could see my coach and the girls from my group standing around me. Looking down at my feet, I could see the handsome stranger from the hall standing there a couple of feet away looking at me. Then I blinked my eyes, and he was gone. I sat up very slowly. Looking around to see if he were still there, I saw he was nowhere in sight.

"Are you okay?" My coach knelt down beside me. She helped me stand to my feet.

"Yes, I'm okay."

"You're sure?"

"Yes, I'm fine. I'm just going to sit and rest for a little while."

"Okay, you take your time," the coach said. "Okay, ladies, up in pyramids. Let's go!"

Walking over by the gate, I sat down up against it while looking back up into the bleachers. I then noticed that Kyle was still there sitting in the bleachers, but the stranger wasn't. *Did I literally hit my head that hard that I imagined him standing there?*

Even as I looked confused, I knew what I thought I saw wasn't really what I saw. Or was it?

After practice, I went back to the locker room to grab my things.

Walking to my car, Amy caught up with me and stopped me in my path. "Did you forget that you were my ride home or what?"

"I'm so sorry. It totally slipped my mind."

"It's okay. I'll just catch a ride with Chelsea."

"Are you sure?"

"Yeah, I understand you had a rough first day."

"Thanks so much," I told her. "I'll call you later."

"Okay," she replied.

Reaching my car, I got into the driver's seat and drove home. I wasn't even thinking to say good-bye to anyone. I wasn't in the mood to hang around school right now.

Pulling up into the driveway to my house, I could see that Aunt Kristen was home by her 2013 Hyundai Genesis in the driveway. Getting out of my car, I felt really light-headed.

"Gosh, I must have hit my head harder than I thought," I said to myself while carefully walking up the stairs to the porch.

Walking through the front door, I could hear Aunt Kristen in the kitchen. Dropping my bag by the door, I continued my way into the kitchen. Kristen was getting dinner ready. She was fixing my favorite, four-cheese lasagna.

"Hey," I said in a very tired voice while sitting down at the counter.

"Hey, sweetie. How was your day at school?"

"It was okay, not exactly how I imagined my first day of senior year being, but we all can't get what we want."

"That bad, huh?" While she still cut up tomatoes. "You want to talk about it?"

"Not really," I said with a very aggravated look on my face.

I just want to forget about the whole day, except one part, meeting that handsome stranger I bumped into. I had a very small smile on my face.

"What's all this for?" I asked.

"Well, I know tomorrow is your big eighteenth birthday, and I just thought that we could have one last dinner as you being my little girl before turning into an adult tomorrow."

"Wow, thank you so much. Just because I'm turning eighteen tomorrow doesn't mean that I'm not going to need you in my life as much as I already do. I'm going to always need you, Aunt Kristen."

Tears filled her eyes. Smiling at me, she walked from behind the counter and hugged me dearly. "Okay, you go upstairs and get cleaned up. I will call you down when your big dinner is ready." She gently wiped away her tears from her cheeks.

I shook my head okay, went to the front door, grabbed my bag, and walked upstairs to my room. Entering my room brought a very relaxed feeling throughout my body. The first day of school was so emotional in so many different ways. I was just happy that it was over.

CHAPTER 5

I walked to the other side of my room to put my things on my desk. Heading over to my bathroom, I got undressed to take a shower. My clothes hit the floor one by one. Turning on the water, I could feel the steam from the shower hitting every part of my body that was not covered. Stepping inside of the shower, I felt the showerhead making the water touch my body so flowingly. The water covered every inch of my body from head to toe. I started to feel more relaxed and less stressed.

After about thirty minutes in the shower, I cut off the water, stepped out of the shower, and reached for my towel. Wrapping it around me to dry off, I reached for another towel to dry my hair.

While drying my hair with the towel, I walked out of the bathroom. I got a few steps out and looked at my window where, out of the corner of my eye, I saw Kyle climbing through the window to my bedroom.

I jumped in surprise. "Oh my goodness! You scared me, Kyle."

"I'm sorry. I didn't mean to."

"It's fine. Just stay right there so I can get dressed."

Walking behind my Japanese-style room divider, I got dressed.

"So I got some great movies for us to watch," Kyle said.

"Am I really watching my best friend get dressed?" he said to himself. He could see the shadow of my body behind my room divider as I got dressed. He was literally in a daze.

Putting the last piece of clothing onto my body, I walked from behind my room divider. I glanced at Kyle, and he was just staring at me in a very weird way.

"Why are you staring at me like that?" I asked.

Standing there in front of my window, he just smiled at me.

"Kyle," I said with a confused look.

Finally, as his lips spread apart, words began to leave his mouth. "No reason. Just daydreaming. What movie should we watch first? Vampires or zombies?"

Pulling the movies from his bag, Kyle and I both looked at each other, and with large smiles on our faces, we both screamed out "Zombies!" at the same time. I jumped onto my bed. Kyle walked over to the television to put on the movie. Walking to the foot of my bed, Kyle turned around and sat on the floor.

Grabbing his bag off the floor, he dumped out all kinds of junk food on the floor.

"Oooh, Sour Twizzlers," I said.

"I know it's your favorite," he said.

Grabbing the Twizzlers, he handed them to me.

"Thanks," I told him.

Taking a bite out of one, I couldn't help but smile at him. As the movie started to play, Aunt Kristen knocked on the door.

"Come in," I said.

She opened the door and noticed Kyle and me watching a movie. "Hi, Kyle. I didn't realize you were here."

"Hello, Mrs. Thompson. I climbed through the window."

"Oh, okay. Well, I just came up to let you know that dinner is ready," Aunt Kristen said.

"Okay, but is it okay if we eat it in here tonight?" I asked.

"Sure, just don't forget to clean up afterward, okay?"

"All right," I answered. "Come on, Kyle. Let's go get our plates."

"No, it's okay. I will bring them to you. You two just sit and watch your movie."

"Okay, thanks," I replied to her.

She smiled at me and closed the door behind her.

"Your aunt is so cool," Kyle said to me.

I glanced over to look at him with a confused expression on my face. "What do you mean?"

"Well, you know, a guy climbing through your window and not even knowing he's in the room."

"Well, you're not just some guy climbing through my window. You're my best friend. And she knows nothing will ever happen between us."

"Yeah, you're right." Kyle had a very small smirk on his face.

A knock came to the door.

"Come in."

"Here are your plates and drinks," said Kristen.

Kyle got up to take the tray away from her. "Thank you."

"You're welcome, sweetie. Well, I will leave you two alone. You guys have fun and don't stay up too late."

"Okay, we won't," I told her.

"Good night, sweetheart," she said to me.

"Good night." I got up to give her a hug.

"Good night, Kyle."

"Good night, Mrs. Thompson."

She smiled back at me and left my room.

Kyle and I began eating and watching the movie. While eating, Kyle grabbed the remote for the television and pressed pause.

"Hey, why did you do that?"

"You are sure you're okay with breaking up with Tyler?" He put all of his attention on me.

I stared down at my plate for a second. I couldn't help but feel bad from the question Kyle just asked me. "Yes. Look, I know I hurt him, and I told myself I would never do that. However, I had to break up with him, Kyle. I love him, but I'm not in love with him. Tyler is a good guy, and he deserves better. You know, it's really weird how the person you think you're going to end up with turns out to be the person you don't end up with. Even so, it's for the best."

"You're correct, Nichole. You did the right thing. I just hope I find someone too."

"It would really suck if I were doomed to never be happy with someone." I looked down at my hands.

Grabbing my hand, Kyle looked at me with a very soft smile on his face. "You're not going to be alone, Nichole. You have too many beautiful qualities to be by yourself."

"You really think so? I don't think I know. Besides, as long as I'm here, you'll never be alone. Thank you, Kyle. You always know what to say."

"Any time." He smiled.

I sat there on my bed and thought about what Kyle just said to me. The next thing that came into my mind was the guy I ran into in the hall today. Just thinking of his hazel brown eyes and the way they stared into mine made me feel weak. *He didn't even seem real to me. He looked too perfect to be unimaginable. I wonder if Kyle knows anything about him.*

Looking at me, Kyle could tell something was on my mind. "What is it? You look like you want to say something."

"It's nothing," I told him.

"No, just tell me. I want to know."

"Have you seen that new kid around school?"

"Yeah, I know who you are talking about. No one knows who he is or what his story is. All the girls in AP chemistry were talking about him today. He seems like a conceited guy to me. No one I would know wants to hang out with him." He then stared at me with a very confused look upon his face. "Why do you ask?"

"Just curious. That's all."

"Well, from what I have heard, he is from here. He used to live here. Everyone says that he moved back to Jackson Pete because he was homesick. He seems weird to me, like he can't be trusted. I even heard that he has no parents and lives alone."

"That's so depressing."

"I guess it is sad. Why do you want to know this stuff?"

"I told you that I was just curious."

"Okay," replied Kyle in a very strange way.

We finished eating and took our plates to the kitchen. After cleaning up after ourselves in the kitchen, we both headed back upstairs. Walking into my room, Kyle and I continued watching the movie. While watching the film for about twenty minutes, I looked down at Kyle, and he was asleep on the floor.

I couldn't help but smile just to realize how lucky I was to have such a great best friend. I got up to turn off the light but kept the television going to finish the movie. I glanced over at my clock and saw that it was eleven thirty-five.

Wow. Time really flew by.

CHAPTER 6

While watching the remainder of the film, I drifted off into a nice, comfortable sleep. Deeper into my sleep, I began to dream. I could see footsteps pressing into the dirt, leaving shoe prints while running through the woods. The speed alone was hard to see. It seemed as though they were running away from something, trying to stay alive. While running, a body shape of a man appeared in front of the footsteps.

Finally, I could see a man and women standing side by side. In front of them was a tall but very slim, muscular man. I couldn't see his face, but he had on a very nice suit. I could see the tall man grab both of them by the neck, lifting them both up off the ground and into the air. I then saw their eyes begin to turn blue. A blue crystal floated off a string tied around the woman's slim neck. A very powerful energy began to be sucked out of their bodies and into the blue crystal. I could feel myself slowly begin to start lifting off my mattress and into the air, floating above my bed while dreaming. The crazy thing was that I couldn't wake myself up.

As the energy was continuously being sucked out of them both, I could feel energy building inside of me, making my whole body inside and outside feel like it was on fire. The energy alone began to light up my entire room, waking up Kyle.

Opening his eyes, he got up off the floor and backed up into the wall in complete disbelief in what was happening. Making himself snap out of his disbelief, he ran to grab Nichole. However, the energy surrounding her shot him back into the wall. The force from the energy was so strong that it kept him up against the wall, not being able to move any inch of his body.

"Nichole!" Kyle yelled repeatedly. "Wake up!"

I could hear Kyle, but I couldn't answer him at all. My body was just frozen. I could feel an extremely painful sensation in my inner left wrist begin to form. The feeling was very intense. It felt like someone was carving into my skin with a sharp knife and all, though I could still feel every single piece of the pain. I, at the same time, couldn't move.

I could hear the man in the suit chanting words. It sounded as if he were speaking Latin. As he chanted the words, the power from the crystal was passed from her crystal into his crystal around his neck. I could see the fear in their eyes as they both knew what was next. With one move in his hands he broke their necks, letting them go they fall to the ground with no life in their dead bodies. I could hear footsteps coming down the hallway and rushing to my room door. Someone was trying to turn the doorknob to get in, but the door would not budge. I could hear a woman's voice screaming my name in fright, just completely terrified in the event that was happening. I noticed the voice, and it was Aunt Kristen. I could hear things falling off the shelves in my room. My pictures and posters were shaking and falling off the walls.

Outside of my window, a person was standing outside, looking up at my room window. The mysterious stranger stood there for a few seconds and then ran quickly away from the house.

A car pulled up into the driveway. Rushing, Uncle Matthew stepped out of his car, and he was in complete surprise and confusion of what he was seeing. He could hear the screaming coming from inside the house. Quickly running inside to see what was going on, he reached the top of the stairs. He turned to the right and saw Kristen trying to get into my room.

He ran to her and tried to kick down the door, but still it would not budge. I could hear everything around me but could not do anything about it. Suddenly, I felt my body slowly begin to lower down to my bed. I could feel the soft pillow touch of my mattress begin to trace every part of my backside.

I could feel the pain easing up through my body until the point I couldn't feel anything. I could feel everything around me stop shaking. And after what seemed like forever, I came out of my dreamlike state, quickly opening my eyes. I sat up, gasping for air. I was completely out of control with fear. Kyle fell onto the floor, and he was frozen in fear against the wall.

The door to my room flew open. Kristen and Matthew ran in and over to me.

"Oh my God! What just happened? Are you okay?" Kristen said, all the while holding me in her arms.

Matthew ran over to Kyle to see if he were okay. Kyle jumped back from his touch. Taking a quick look at me, I could see the fear in his eyes, just blank and in confusion, but so helpless and scared at the same time. He stood up on his two feet and ran out of the house.

"Kyle, wait!" yelled Uncle Matthew as he ran after him.

CHAPTER 7

I couldn't stop the pain I felt in my heart for those two people I saw die in my dream. *Why did I dream of them, and what in the hell just happened to me?*

"What is going on?" I asked.

"I don't know, sweetie. Let's go downstairs, and we can discuss it there," said Aunt Kristen.

Walking downstairs, I sat down at the kitchen table. My mind couldn't process what just happened to me upstairs. Deep in shock, we all just sat there in silence. Not knowing exactly what to say or how to start a conversation, Aunt Kristen wouldn't even look up at me. She just stared down at the table, completely lost in thought. It seemed as if she had something on her mind, something she was just dying to get out. After what seemed like forever, she spoke to me with the calmest voice that would make anyone feel safe.

I couldn't help but smile at her when she said to me, "Would you like some tea, sweetheart?"

"Sure, that would be great."

She very flowingly got up from the table and began to fix the tea. Uncle Matthew got up from the table to get a blanket off the couch and brought it over to me to cover me up.

"Thank you," I said.

He walked back to his seat and sat down at the table in front of me. "Are you sure you're okay?"

"I don't know," I replied. "I don't even know what happened."

Kristen walked up behind me and put a cup of tea in front of me.

"Thank you," I said to her.

She smiled and sat down in front of me at the table beside Matthew.

"What happened to Kyle?" I asked.

Matthew took a deep sigh before answering. He was extremely terrified. "The look in his eyes was so blank that you would have thought he had seen a ghost. I tried to run after him, but he was already gone when I reached the bottom of the stairs." He paused for a few seconds. "Nichole, what happened in your room?"

I could feel the tension at the table with that one question. I knew they just wanted to know what really happened behind my room door. *Nevertheless, how could I tell them what actually happened to me, the pain I felt, and what my body was doing? How could I tell them without sounding crazy? I can't tell them. I'm just going to share with them what they need to know.*

I took a deep breath and told them the short version but without the craziness. "I was dreaming."

"Dreaming?" asked Matthew with a very confused look on his face.

"So you didn't feel the house shaking, and I saw a bright light from underneath your door," said Kristen.

"I was not aware of any of that," I replied.

"Okay, sweetheart. It's fine. Just tell us what happened before you fell asleep, leading up to the dream you had," said Matthew.

"After dinner, Kyle and I brought our dishes into the kitchen. We cleaned up after ourselves, headed back to my room, and started watching a movie. I remember seeing Kyle asleep on the floor. I got up to turn off the light and laid back down in my bed. I dozed off after that." I looked confused.

I could feel Matthew's eyes glued on me.

"What is it, Nichole?" Matthew asked me.

I paused for a quick second. "It's just my dream. This wasn't the first time I've dreamed about it."

"Well, what was the dream about?" asked Kristen.

"I saw two people, a male and a female, running. They were running through the woods. A man came out of nowhere, and before they could do anything, he grabbed them and killed them both. It felt so real to me like I was there, like I was connected to them both somehow."

Finishing up my story, I looked up at my aunt and uncle. I saw a very pale but shocked look of guilt on their faces. The look on their faces gave me chills. *What could possibly be the cause of this expression on their faces?*

I couldn't hold my tongue for much longer. I had to know. I looked both of them straight into their eyes. "What's wrong with you two? Why are you guys looking at me like that?"

Kristen slowly grabbed my hands and put them inside of hers firmly. Then with a very light voice, she began to talk to me. "Nichole, I think you were having a memory, sweetheart."

"What do you mean? A memory?" I had a very confused look on my face.

There was a very long pause in the room. Uncle Matthew grabbed a chair, pulled it next to me, and sat down beside me. He put his arm around my shoulder and gently put his hand on top of Kristen's that was on top of mine. "Your parents were not killed in a car accident, Nichole," he said with a hesitant presence in his voice. "We found you in the woods when you were a baby. Your Aunt Kristen and I were out camping and heard someone screaming while lying in the tent. I got up and went to look around to see what was going on. As I went deeper into the woods, I began to see footprints on the ground, so I followed them. The footprints led me to a log covered in moth and surrounded by leaves. I began removing the leaves away from the log, and inside the log, I found a baby wrapped in a blanket."

Kristen let go of my hands while getting up from the table. She walked over to the side closet and grabbed an ivory blanket from the top shelf. She brought it to the table and gently slid it in front of me.

The blanket had dingy edges but was soft as cotton. It had a symbol on it that looked very familiar to me. I put my right hand out to grab the blanket. The closer my hand got to the blanket, the stronger my fear became to knowing the truth. I quickly pulled away my hand and put it down to my side.

"What are you two trying to tell me?" Tears filled my eyes.

"Sweetheart, you were the baby I found in the woods."

I quickly stood up from the table. "You're lying!"

"We wanted to tell you sooner," he said.

"No, you didn't," I replied. "You just lied instead."

"Nichole, we knew we could not compare to your real parents. We thought we were doing the right thing. That's why we told you that we were your aunt and uncle." Tears were rushing down Kristen's face as she reached out to hug me.

Even so, how could I let her touch me? How could I trust them anymore? Do I really know who they are? I can't do this. I just can't.

"Don't touch me." I backed up defensively away from her. "I don't know who you two really are anymore."

"Don't say that, sweetie." Kristen pleaded.

I looked over to her with hatred in my eyes. "Why not? It's true. You two have been dishonest with me my whole life. Wait, your last name is Thompson. Whose last name do I have? You told me it was my father's last name."

"No, sweetheart," said Matthew. "Gibson is your Aunt Kristen's maiden name."

What type of people would lie like that? I stormed out of the kitchen and ran upstairs into my room. *What is happening to my life right now?*

Grabbing my bag, I packed some clothes. Gripping my keys and cell phone, I then stormed out of my room and went back downstairs.

Kristen saw me heading out of the door. "Where are you going, Nichole?" she asked in a very concerned voice.

Turning the doorknob and slightly opening the door, I stood there for a second. Slowly, I turned around to face them both.

"That's none of your business anymore."

I pulled the door wide open and slammed the door behind me. Driving my car out of the driveway, I could see Kristen and Matthew running out of the door and down the porch stairs to catch me. Unfortunately, they were too late.

Looking into my rearview mirror, I could see Kristen falling into Matthew's arms, telling me to wait and to let her explain. However, I couldn't stand to be around them right now. So how could I possibly try to talk to the both of them?

"We've lost her, Matt. We've lost our baby." Kristen continued crying into his arms.

Not having anything to say, he just held her tight and cried with her in thought that their family was now and forever never going to be the same.

CHAPTER 8

Driving down a long, dark road, all I could feel was pain. The tears in my eyes felt so heavy. The pain in my heart made me feel as if my heart were going to break in half. *I have to call Amy and ask if it's okay to stay with her for a couple of days.*

I knew it would be okay. She practically stayed by herself. Her parents were always gone, out of town for business. Dialing Amy's number, I could hear the phone begin to ring. *Please pick up.*

After four rings, a very tired and crackly voice came through the phone. "Hello?"

"Amy, I'm so sorry to call this late, but I didn't know who else to call. Is it okay if I come over?" I asked.

"Sure, I'll leave the door unlocked. Just come up to my room," she said.

"Okay, I'll be there in about ten minutes," I replied.

"Are you okay?" she asked. "You sound really upset."

"I'll explain everything when I get there."

"Okay," she said.

Hanging up the phone, I dropped it on the car floor. Bending down to pick it up, I took my eyes off the road for a quick second. As my eyes returned on the road, I saw a guy standing in the middle of the road. I hit the brakes quickly, and the car swerved to come to a complete stop. I got out of the car to find no one there, just me standing in the middle of the road alone.

"What the hell? Is anyone out here?" I yelled.

But no one answered. *I could have sworn I saw a guy standing there. I know I'm not going crazy, or am I?*

Standing there in the road was giving me the creeps. Rushing, I got back into my car and drove to Amy's house. Pulling up to her house, I could see both of her parents' cars were gone. This meant she was home alone, and I knew it would be okay.

Turning off the car, I sat in my seat for a few seconds. *Why is this all happening to me?*

Grabbing my bag, I got out of the car and walked into Amy's house. She was standing right there in the front entrance.

Closing the door behind me, I couldn't do anything but stand there. Looking right at her, I could feel tears begin to fill my eyes. Falling to my knees, I looked up at her with so much pain in my eyes.

"Are you okay?" She knelt down beside me.

"No," I replied while crying.

"Here, let's go upstairs, and we will talk about it in my room."

Nodding my head in agreement, we stood to our feet and walked upstairs and into her room. Keeping her arm around me, she told me that everything was going to be okay. Sitting down on her bed, I reached for one of her pillows. Pulling it close into my chest, I had to sit there for a moment.

Then out of nowhere, I just began telling her everything. "My aunt and uncle have been dishonest with me my whole life."

"What do you mean?"

"Well, to sum it all up, my real parents did not die in a car crash. My aunt and uncle found me in a log in the woods. I'm adopted, Amy."

"Oh my goodness, Nichole. I am so sorry. I can't even imagine. Good thing you don't have to."

"I feel very betrayed and confused."

"So did they just come out and tell you?"

"Not exactly. I had this dream tonight. It's the same dream I've been having for the past couple of nights now."

"So what was the dream about?"

"It starts off the same with two people, a man and a woman, running from something in the woods. Then suddenly, a tall man is standing in front of them and grabs their necks, lifting them off the ground." Looking up at Amy, I in that very second remembered something from my dream.

"Nichole, what is it?"

"On the woman's neck, she had a necklace with a blue crystal on it. I remember all the energy being sucked out of their bodies. The fear in their eyes seemed unbearable. All of that energy was being sucked into another blue crystal around the tall man's neck." Taking a deep breath, I stood up and walked to her window. "I felt something happen to me as I was dreaming tonight. It felt like I was floating, and I could hear things shaking and falling in my room, but for some reason, I couldn't move or wake myself up. I also felt like I was on fire."

"Nichole, not to be funny, but floating and feeling like you were on fire really sounds a little crazy."

"Yeah, but it felt so real, Amy. All I know is that, when I came out of it, Kyle was looking at me like he was afraid of me, and my aunt was holding me as I was screaming, trying to calm me down."

"Nichole, look at me," Amy said. "It was just a dream."

"No, it wasn't. According to Matthew and Kristen, it was a memory."

"What do you mean?" she asked.

"By me explaining to them, that dream made them tell me the truth about how they found me. They showed me the blanket they found me in and everything." Walking back over to Amy, I sat down next to her, moving my hair from my face. "I have no idea what to do. Do I talk to them? Do I avoid them? I just don't know."

Taking my hand into hers, she gave me a very comforting smile. "You know what to do, Nichole. Just sleep on it. Get your thoughts together. You know you are always welcome to stay here. You are like a sister to me."

"Thank you, Amy. You're a great friend."

"I know I am. Plus, tomorrow is your birthday, and you know we have to celebrate."

Looking up at her, I smiled while giving her a hug.

"You just get some sleep, okay?"

Nodding my head in agreement with her, I laid down on her bed. I closed my eyes. *I hope tomorrow will be better.* I drifted into a deep sleep.

Waking up the next morning, I had hoped everything that happened to me last night was nothing but a bad dream. Nevertheless, waking up in Amy's room quickly brought me back to reality. It certainly showed me that it was not a bad dream at all but reality.

Kristen and Matthew had been calling me nonstop. I couldn't possibly talk to them right know. I just wasn't ready for that yet. Driving that morning to school was very silent. I truly didn't feel like going. Nevertheless, I seriously needed to see Kyle. I just wanted to know if he were okay.

Driving into the school parking lot, my phone rang. I glanced at it while putting my car in park. It was Uncle Matthew calling me again. I couldn't talk to him right now, and to tell the truth, pressing ignore on the phone gave me a little relief.

Amy noticed me ignoring his call and looked very concerned. "You are sure you're okay?"

"I just can't talk to them right now. I'm not ready for that yet. I just want to get today over with."

"Well, if that's what you want, then do that. Even so, we are going to celebrate your birthday today."

"Okay." I smiled at her as we both got out of the car.

Walking into the school hallway, I glanced at Kyle's locker. I noticed no one was there. *He must be avoiding me. I don't blame him at all. I really hope he is okay.*

Continuing to walk beside Amy, we reached the end of the hall. Turning the corner, I suddenly felt a sharp pain in my inner left wrist.

"Ouch! What the hell was that?" I said to myself while stopping in my path.

Grabbing my inner left wrist, I looked down to see if everything were okay. I noticed I had the same symbol from my blanket on my skin. I could remember feeling a huge amount of pain that night from my inner wrist. It felt as though someone was carving into my skin with a sharp knife. *What did this mean? I couldn't let anyone see this.*

"Are you okay?" Amy asked.

"Yes, I'm fine. I will see you in class."

"Okay." Amy had a very confused look upon her face as I walked off.

I covered up the symbol with my right hand and continued to walk to my locker. "What is happening to me?" I asked myself. I closed my eyes and took a deep breath and exhaled as I stood in front of my locker. "You're fine. Everything is going to be fine," I told myself.

Opening my locker door, I began to reach for my book and paused as I glanced to my right at the inside of my locker door. With sadness rushing through my veins, I continued to look at the picture of Kyle and me taped on the inside of my locker door. Rolling my eyes, I grabbed my book and slammed my locker door shut.

I couldn't help but wish Kyle was right here with me, telling me everything would be okay. I needed my best friend more than ever, and he was nowhere to be found. He wouldn't even answer any of my phone calls. I felt all alone, so much like an outcast.

I saw Amy and Chelsea walking over to me out of the corner of my eyes.

"Are you okay? Amy told me everything. I hope that was okay," said Chelsea.

"Yes, it's fine. I want you to know. I don't want to think about it right now. I just want to get through today."

"It sounds great to me. Let's go to class. Just to let you know, whatever you need, it's yours," said Chelsea.

"Thank you guys so much for being there for me."

All they could do was smile at each other.

"Anytime. Now let's hurry to class before we're late," said Amy.

Smiling at them both, I continued to walk into class with them.

Walking into the classroom, I sat right at my desk. Sitting down at my desk felt so different to me. It felt as if I didn't belong there anymore, even at school for that matter. I felt so out of place, and as I sat there, every single thing that happened to me last night was in my head all at once. *The people I called family turned out not to be. Why do I have this symbol on my inner wrist? What happened to me when I was asleep? Even though I could not see anything, I could feel everything. Why did I have that dream? What did it mean?*

Everything rushing in my head all at once was too much. I just wanted and needed it all to stop.

CHAPTER 9

I couldn't take all those thoughts in my head at the same time. With panic taking over my body, I rushed out of the classroom, leaving everything behind. Not even caring what the consequences would be, I continued to run through the halls of the school. Bursting through the double doors at the back of the school, I kept running.

With tears rolling down my cheeks, I continued running, only feeling hopelessness, despair, and neglect, not freedom or happiness. I ran through the student parking lot, passed the football field, and made it into the woods. I could feel every step that I made dig into the ground. I didn't stop until I could no longer run because there was no ground left to run on. It was only me standing all alone at the edge of a cliff. I felt the cold wind go through every string of my dark brown hair. My caramel skin got chills from the coldness of the air.

Standing there at the edge of the cliff, all I knew was that I wanted all the pain to go away. I couldn't take it anymore. I thought I was okay, but the truth of the matter was that I wasn't. Looking down beneath my feet, I could see the waves rushing to the walls of the cliff. I didn't want to live anymore. I had nothing to live for. *Everything about me was a lie.*

Closing my eyes, I leaned forward off the cliff to fall to my death. Gravity was pulling me down fast. I could feel my body start to relax, preparing itself for the impact. *This is it?*

Suddenly, I felt a hand on my shoulder and an arm wrapping around my waist. Then the pull of gravity stopped. I felt myself laying on a hard, flat surface, and I could feel the weight of someone on top of me.

Opening my eyes very slowly, I began to notice a face. "Am I dead?" I asked in a crackling voice.

"No, you're not dead," the stranger said.

Hiding my face in my hands, I broke down in tears.

"Are you okay?" he asked.

"No, I'm not. Why did you stop me?" I rushed to the edge. "I can't take my life anymore."

"Okay, just calm down."

"No, I can't take this anymore. I have to end it."

"Wait, let's just talk, okay?" the stranger said to me. "Look, if nothing that we talk about helps you, I will not stop you. However, please just let me try to help you."

Turning around to face him, I wiped away my tears. "You're the guy from the hall."

"Yeah, why are you trying to do this to yourself?" he asked.

I took two steps away from the edge and tried to get my thoughts together. I wondered how he knew I was out here. "What the hell are you doing out here? Did you follow me or something?"

"Calm down, okay? And yes, I did. I saw you running across the football field from the bleachers with tears in your eyes. You looked so upset, and I just wanted to see if you were okay. It's a good thing I did follow you because you were obviously really upset."

"You know what? This does not concern you. You don't even know what I've been through."

"Well, I'm pretty sure it's not enough to want to kill yourself over."

"Why do you care anyway?" I asked.

"Look, you're right, I don't know you, and I don't know what you are upset about. Nevertheless, I do know that you need someone to talk to. And I'll sit right here with you and talk as long as you want."

"Why would you do that?"

"Because whatever kind of pain you're going though, you don't have to make it go away like this."

Looking into his eyes, I couldn't feel anything but comfort. And in truth, I needed all the comfort I could get. "Okay." I walked slowly toward him. "I don't even know where to start."

"Come sit and start wherever you want," he said to me.

"Okay." I wiped away my tears and took a seat next to him. "Well, for starters, last night was the worst night of my life."

"Why so?" he asked.

Taking a deep breath, I let out a long sigh. "I found out my aunt and uncle are not who they say they are."

"What do you mean?"

"Let's just say I've been lied to all my life. My whole life is a lie." Tears formed in my eyes. "My best friend won't even talk to me. I have no plans for my future. Oh, yeah, and to top it off, today is my eighteenth birthday. Look at me. I'm so pathetic. Here I am telling a stranger my sad story. You must think I'm a freak."

"No, actually the complete opposite. And I would hardly consider me a stranger. I mean, you have seen me before. And to tell you the truth, I like listening to you."

A very pleasant but calm feeling came over me. I couldn't help but smile back at him.

"You know, we are talking to each other, but we don't even know each other's names." Turning around to face me, he smiled at me. "I'm Isaac Carter." He held out his hand for me to shake it.

"I'm Nichole Gibson." I shook his hand. "So where are you from?"

"I'm actually from here. I've just been traveling a lot. I've been homeschooled most of my life. Even so, I thought to change it up a little. I mean, you only get one senior year in high school, right?"

"Yeah, too bad mine isn't going exactly as planned. Maybe not now, but I'm sure it will get better. I could only hope," I replied with a tiny smirk.

"So have you lived here long?" he asked.

"I've lived here my whole life. Well, at least I think I have. What do your parents do that makes you travel so much?"

40

"Actually, it's just me. My parents died when I was very young."

"I'm so sorry."

"It's okay. I just had to grow up a lot faster than others."

"If you don't mind me asking, where have you traveled?" I asked.

"Okay, how about this? Name a place, and I'll say yes if I've been there and no if I haven't."

"Okay, how about Paris?" I asked.

"Yes, three times actually."

"Wow, I bet it's beautiful there. I've always wanted to go there. Just to swim in the oceans and walk through the streets at night. Eating a romantic candlelit dinner on a balcony with breathtaking views of the Eiffel Tower. The culture in general takes my breath away." Closing my eyes, I couldn't do anything but smile to the thought of me being there. It made me feel at peace.

Looking over at her, I'd never seen anyone or anything so beautiful in my life. Watching her embrace in her thoughts was so peaceful. She looked so beautiful and full of life.

"You never know. Maybe you will someday," he said.

"I doubt it. It's just a dream anyway. It's not like I will actually go."

As he glanced over at me, he smiled. "Never say never."

There was something about him that was so consuming. Looking into his eyes, I could have sworn that my heart had skipped a beat. There was a short but pleasant pause between us. We both looked into each other's eyes, not even realizing that the more we talked to each other, the closer we became to each other.

Out of nowhere, my phone rang. Coming out of the daze I was in, I reached in my back pocket and grabbed my phone. Looking down at my phone, I noticed a missed call from Amy.

"I'm sorry. It's my friend Amy. I should call her back. She's probably wondering what happened to me."

Standing to his feet beside me, he reached out for my hand to help me up. Smiling, I accepted his invitation and stood up in front of him, close to his body.

"I'm sorry. I didn't mean to get so close."

"It's okay. I don't mind," he said.

Looking up at him, I couldn't help but smile.

"Would you like to walk back to the school with me?" I asked with a very flirty tone in my voice.

"Sure, I would really like that," Isaac replied. "I mean, we're both going to the same place."

Walking out of the woods into the open football field in the back of the school, we both stopped in our steps to face each other.

"Okay, even if I don't see you again after this, there is something I want to say to you. You are a wonderful person. You shouldn't want to end your life just because it's a little difficult right now. Remember this. It's the obstacles and mistakes that make us the person that we are destined to be. And trust me, from what I see, you are very special, and a person like you should never feel that ending your life is the way. It might hurt now. Even so, the pain will go away."

Looking up at him, I could feel a tear roll down my cheek. "You're right, and thank you so much for being there for me. You're a nice guy."

"Well, I wouldn't say that. I'm a likeable guy."

"What? You're not a nice guy?" I asked.

"Of course not," Isaac replied. "I actually think I'm a great guy."

I smiled at him and looked down at the ground. "Hopefully, I will see you around."

"Just take it a day at a time. Hey, look at me."

Lifting my chin in his hand so gently, I met his eyes with mine.

"You're going to be fine."

As much as I wanted to believe him, everything inside me was telling me otherwise. "I should get back to class."

"Okay, I guess I'll see you around," he said.

Standing there, he watched as I walked away. I turned around and smiled back at him. I owed Isaac my life. I was so grateful for what he did. He really made me feel better about myself. *But how did he stop me from falling? I felt myself falling. Then suddenly I wasn't.*

Walking back into school, I noticed Amy and Chelsea standing by my locker with my things.

Walking up to them, Amy grabbed me and hugged me. "Are you okay?"

"I'm a lot better now. I'm just going to put my stuff in my locker."

"Okay, when you're done, come meet us in the lunchroom."

"Wow, it's time for lunch already."

"Yeah, you missed first and second period."

"Well, I'll meet you guys in the lunchroom."

"Okay," said Amy.

After putting up my things, I headed to the lunchroom to look for Amy and Chelsea. I walked over to get in line to get something to eat. Out of nowhere, I heard someone say "hey" in my ear.

Jumping out of fright, I turned around to notice Kyle behind me. "You, jackass. You scared me."

"Sorry. I didn't mean to scare you. How are you doing?"

"How do you think I'm doing?"

"Look, Nichole, I'm sorry for leaving the way I did. I was just really freaked out."

"You didn't think that I wasn't, Kyle? I'm still freaked out about everything."

"Look, I don't want to argue with you. I just wanted to come over here and tell you that I ran into Amy, and she filled me in about your aunt and uncle."

"Oh," I said while cutting him off. "So is that the only reason that you're over here talking to me right now? Let me ask you something, Kyle. If you didn't know, would you be over here talking to me right now?"

"Why would you even ask me that? No, better yet, why are you acting like this toward me?"

"Because, Kyle, you're my best friend. I needed you, and for the first time in the most critical and worst situation I have ever been in, you were not there for me, not at all. You have no idea what I have been going through. And what I tried to do to myself because I felt so alone."

"Wait, what did you try to do to yourself?"

"It's none of your business."

"Nichole, just tell me."

"I tried to kill myself, okay?"

The look that appeared on his face was so pale. Looking in his eyes, I could tell that I knew he regretted not being there for me.

"Now if you will excuse me, I have to go find my real friends."

Walking away from Kyle was very hard to do. Even though I was upset with him, I still very much needed his friendship.

"Nichole!" Kyle yelled.

"What?" I replied back.

"Happy birthday," he said and walked out of the lunchroom.

CHAPTER 10

Walking over to the table, I sat down next to Amy and felt everyone's eyes on me. It made me feel so uncomfortable.

"I have to go, guys. Amy, I will see you at your house."

I grabbed my bag and walked out the double lunchroom doors, heading straight toward my car. As I reached my car, I noticed Isaac was sitting on the hood of my car. All of my discomfort faded away while walking up to him.

"Why are you sitting on my car? How did you even know this was mine?"

"I have my ways of getting information at this school."

"Oh, really?"

Sliding off the hood, he walked up to me and smiled. "Will you go somewhere with me?"

"Where?"

"I can't tell you were. Nevertheless, I promise you will like it."

Looking very confused at his question, somehow I trusted him more than I've ever trusted anyone in my life. I grabbed his hand and shook my head in agreement.

While riding in the car with Isaac, I couldn't help but gaze at him once in a while from the passenger seat. The way his clothes fit his athletic body was very sexy to me. I could see every curve in his arms. Every turn of his arms on the steering wheel would make his muscles flex through his shirt. His pants fit the lower half of his body so perfectly. *Wait a minute? Am I really daydreaming about his body right know?*

I had to say something to get my mind off his body. "So are we almost there?"

"Actually, we are here."

The car came to a complete stop. While getting out of the vehicle, I couldn't help but be amazed to what was before my eyes. In front of me was a beautiful field surrounded by mountains. In the middle of the mountain was a waterfall falling into the most peaceful river I had ever seen.

The greenery of the field and mountains was just beautiful. It almost didn't even seem real. The wind and its temperature felt perfect as it flowed on my skin and blew through my hair. The sun was perfectly shining, and the sky was clear. Everything was perfect. It was so beautiful here.

"I didn't even know this place was in this small town," I said.

"Come on. Let's go down and put our feet in the river." He took me by the hand and led me to the river.

As I walked down to the river, I thought to myself. *Is this really happening? Me being here with Isaac was just breathtaking. How could this guy turn my day from horrible to perfect in a matter of minutes?*

He was just truly amazing. Reaching the edge of the river, we both took off our shoes and sat on the edge as we placed our feet in the water. The water was so warm to the touch. The scenery was even more beautiful.

"This is where I like to come to clear my head and take the time to think about my future," Isaac said.

"I can see why. It's just so peaceful here. However, I can't say that I think of my future very often."

"Why not?" he asked with such concern in his voice.

"To tell you the truth, I don't know what I want to do with my life. I'm just really trying to get through today, you know."

"Well, I bet you're going to be great at whatever you decide to do. You're too special not to be a success."

"You think so?"

"Of course, look at you. You're already beautiful, and from what everyone says at school, you're very talented and smart as well."

"Thank you for today."

"Anytime," he replied.

"No, honestly. You truly have changed my outlook on life in one day. You made me see there are things, beautiful things to live for. And no matter how hard things get, there is always someone there to make it better. You saved me, Isaac." I sat there and stared into his eyes. "And for that, I will always be grateful to you." I gently lifted my hand and placed it on his very firm cheek. "Thank you." Lowering my hand back down to my lap, I looked at Isaac. His smile was so beautiful.

We both sat there and smiled at each other. As I cleared my thoughts, I glanced back at the mountains.

"This place is really beautiful," I said.

"Trust me. There are a lot of attractive things that you haven't seen yet. I would love to show you sometime."

I looked at him at the corner of my eyes. With a very warm smile, I replied, "I would like that."

We both just smiled and enjoyed the incredible surroundings around us. We stayed there enjoying the scenery for the rest of that afternoon.

"It's getting late. Maybe we should head back to the school."

"Yeah, I'll take you to your car."

The ride back to my car was quiet but peaceful. Pulling up in the student parking lot right next to my car, he put his car in park. I opened my door and stepped out of his vehicle. Walking over to my car, he met me at my driver's door.

"Thank you again. I really did need to clear my head."

"Anytime," he replied. "So I'll see you later?"

"Yes, I would like that."

Standing there looking into each other's eyes, Isaac leaned in toward me, getting even closer to my lips. Closing my eyes, I felt his soft lips land on my cheek so gently. The touch of his lips sent chills through my whole body that made me stumble a little.

"Are you okay?"

Catching myself, I opened my eyes. "Yeah, I'm fine. My knee just gave out a little. I'm only tired. That's all."

"Oh, okay." He smiled. "Well, good night, Nichole."

"Good night," I replied back while getting into my car.

Driving away, I couldn't believe what had just happened. I felt so drawn to him. And without a doubt, I could feel myself shortly but surely falling in love with him.

I pulled up in Amy's driveway and could see her in her window at her desk. I knew I was going to have a lot of questions to answer.

Walking into Amy's room, she automatically jumped up to hug me. "I was so worried about you, Nichole." She hit me in the arm.

"Ouch."

"Where did you run off to? I even covered for you at school and got all your classwork."

"I'm sorry. Thank you for doing all of that. I was just really stressed and overwhelmed with everything going on in my life."

"Are you okay?"

"Yes, I'm fine. Better than fine actually."

"So where were you?"

"I went for a drive with Isaac."

"Who is Isaac? Wait, the new kid. Are you serious? You don't even know him."

"Yes, I do. Well now I do."

"Well, he is cute though." Amy smiled.

"He is just so sweet, Amy. He seriously is. He honestly made me see life in a different way today."

"Wow," she said, amazed.

"What?" I asked in a confused tone.

"It's just I have never seen you this happy before and so sure of yourself. I don't know what this guy has done to you, but I like it."

"I know I don't know what it is about him."

"You really like him, don't you?"

"I think I more than like him. I know I am falling in love with him. Is it crazy to feel this way so quickly?"

"Not at all. I'm happy for you."

"Thank you."

"So are you going to talk with your aunt and uncle?"

"You know what? I think I'm prepared. No, I know I'm ready. I'll call you tomorrow."

"Wait. Where are you going?"

"Home."

Standing up off her bed, I grabbed my things and headed out the door.

"Wait, you're going over there now?"

"Yes, I have to do this. If I don't, I'll never do it."

"Good luck," Amy said to me.

"Thanks." I went out the front door.

Pulling up into the driveway to my house, I felt a small chill come over me. At that second, I thought about Isaac and his voice whispering to me that I could do this. I got out of the car and walked up the stairs to the front door. Turning the knob, I slowly opened the door and walked through. Closing the door behind me, I walked into the living room to find my aunt and uncle sitting on the couch.

"Hey, I'm sorry to come in unannounced."

They both stood to their feet in shock, not allowing themselves to do anything but smile lightly. Both Aunt Kristen and Uncle Matthew were very grateful to see me.

"Honey, this is your home. You can come whenever you want."

"Look, I thought we could talk, you know, and just get everything out in the open."

"Okay, that sounds like a good idea," said Kristen.

Walking over to the chair to sit in front of them, I had so much anger inside of me. However, I knew I had to control myself to get through this.

"Okay, just start from the beginning," I said.

"Honey, we told you the most part already," said Uncle Matthew.

"Just tell it to me again, please."

"Okay, well, your aunt and I were out camping that night. I went to get more firewood for the fire. When I returned, your aunt and I heard a scream. I told her to go into the tent and stay there until I got back. I walked along a dirt road, and I began to see footprints in the dust. So I followed them, and they led me to a log. Kneeling down, I removed the leaves that were placed over the opening. Inside the log, I found you as a baby. You were wrapped inside the blanket that we showed you at the dinner table, and I took off my jacket and wrapped it around you also. I rushed back to the tent where Kristen was.

"Your aunt was so surprised to see me with a baby in the middle of nowhere. I told her we had to get you to a hospital. We wanted to make sure you were okay. I called 911 and told them we heard a scream in the woods and I had found a baby also. After walking into the hospital, we saw two cops waiting to question us and a nurse who took you back to examine you. I promise you that we already fell in love with you. You were our daughter the moment I held you in my arms.

"After explaining everything that had happened to the police, they told us that they found two bodies, a male and a female, not too far from the log where I had found you. They were your parents, sweetheart. The doctor who examined you said you were fine and asked if we knew what had happened. We explained what happened the same way we told the two cops, and he told us that you could not be left at the hospital alone. So we agreed to raise you as our own. Nevertheless, knowing we could not take the place of your real parents, we decided to have you know us as your aunt and uncle."

"Were you two able to have children?" I asked.

"What does that have to do with anything?" asked Kristen.

"Just answer the question, please," I asked in a very sad, depressed voice.

"No, we cannot have any children."

"So I was only a child you felt sorry for and just so happened to fall into your lap. Just a chance to get a kid." Tears filled my eyes.

"No, not at all, honey," said Kristen. "Nichole, you made us a family, sweetheart. You are a blessing given to us. No matter how you came into our lives, you are a part of us." She stood up and knelt in front of me, grabbing my hands and putting her hand on my cheek. "Nothing can or ever will change that."

I couldn't help but fall into her arms. Uncle Matthew walked over and hugged us both. Right there in that moment, we were a family again. We weren't a perfect one, but we were putting back the pieces.

"We have to take this day by day. Can I come back home?"

"Honey, of course you can. We love you, sweetie."

"Okay, I just need to be alone right now to let everything sink in."

"Sweetheart, you take all the time you need."

I headed over to the stairs. I turned around to look at them both. "I love you, guys."

"We love you too."

As I turned around, I walked upstairs and walked into my room. All I could do was think to myself, *Thank you, Isaac.*

As I entered my room, a very pleasant feeling came over my body. I fell onto my bed and cuddled up with my pillow. *Today started off being the worst day of my life. Then out of nowhere, it turned into the best day of my life, all because of one person. He is truly a guardian angel.*

Closing my eyes, I hugged my pillow even tighter and fell into a much-needed sleep.

CHAPTER 11

The next morning, I got up a lot earlier than I usually did. I felt different in so many ways, more complete, stronger, and more alive. Getting out of bed, I headed over to my bathroom to take a shower.

All of a sudden, a sharp pain went into my inner left wrist, right where the symbol was on my wrist. Grabbing my wrist with my free hand, I dropped to my knees in pain. Wishing for the pain to go away, I felt my eyes begin to burn.

Forcing myself off the floor, I hurried toward the bathroom. Standing in front of the sink, I opened my eyes and looked into the mirror. Staring at myself, I couldn't believe what I was seeing. My eyes were blue, and the symbol on my inner wrist was glowing in the same color. Then all the pain stopped. Slowly, the symbol on my inner wrist faded to its natural color of my skin, and my eyes turned back normal.

"What the hell is happening to me?" I asked myself.

Freaked out from what I just saw, I rushed out of the bathroom and changed into some sweatpants, a tank top, and green hoodie. Putting on my sneakers, I grabbed my phone and keys and exited my room.

Making sure not to wake Kristen and Matthew, I quietly headed out the door for a drive. I needed to go somewhere to clear my head and to think about what had just happened to me. While continuing to drive, a smile emerged on my face as I began to think of Isaac. I drove to the place that Isaac showed me yesterday.

Getting out of the car, I walked to the edge of the river and sat down to enjoy the view. I just wanted to get my thoughts together. Isaac was on my mind a lot. He saved my life yesterday. *What is it about him that makes me feel so complete? He is just so irresistible. I wish he were here with me right now.*

Then out of nowhere, a hand gently tapped my shoulder. I jumped in fright and turned around. There I saw Isaac, handsome as ever, smiling at me.

"You weren't thinking about me, were you?"

"Oh my God! You scared me." I smiled.

"I'm sorry. I didn't mean to scare you."

"It's okay." I wiped my hair from my face. "And to answer your question, yes, I was just thinking about you."

"Oh, really?"

"Yes, honestly. How did you know I was out here? Did you follow me?" I was smirking.

"Technically, I introduced you to this place so you are actually stalking me. Only trying to see if I would show up, huh?" He smiled.

"No, the truth is that I just needed to come somewhere to get my thoughts together. And this was the first place that came to mind. I didn't even get to celebrate my birthday yesterday."

"I'm sorry about that."

"It's okay. I didn't really feel like celebrating anyway."

"Everyone should celebrate their birthday, Nichole."

"I guess."

"You're too hard on yourself. You need to realize you're a wonderful person. I haven't even known you long, and I can already see it."

"You really think so?"

"Yes, I mean I feel like I've known you my whole life. Trust me. I know what you mean."

"I have a best friend named Kyle that I've known since preschool, and I feel more comfortable with you than I do with him right now."

We both just smiled at each other. Suddenly very slowly, I felt Isaac's hand slide on top of mine, holding my hand so softly. Taking in everything from this moment that was forming, I rested my head on his shoulder. Then from out of nowhere, my body felt a very powerful and passionate sensation building up inside of me. Lifting my head off his shoulder, I shifted my weight to my left side so I was facing him.

"Do you feel that?"

"Of course I do."

Sitting there staring into his eyes, I couldn't help but feel a magnetic-like feeling pulling everything inside of me toward him. "Why do I feel so drawn to you?"

While sitting there looking into my eyes very calmly, a smile appeared on his face. He stood up to his feet beside me and held out his hand as an invitation to stand alongside him. I accepted and stood on my feet in front of him.

"Trust me. You will find out when you're ready," he said to me.

I couldn't help but look confused from what he had just said. He slowly placed my cheek in the palm of his hand and used his other hand to gently lift my chin so I could look him straight into his eyes.

"I'm going to kiss you," he said in the softest voice.

Lost in this moment of passion, I was lost for words. Not wanting to seem uninterested, I opened my mouth and trusted the words that came out next. I would kiss back. He slowly pulled me in closer to him, not leaving any chance for any air to come between us. As the tips of our noses touched, my mouth opened, anxiously awaiting for our lips to connect.

As I closed my eyes, I could feel his lips gently connecting with mine. His lips were so soft and warm. They fit perfectly with mine. His hand gently moved from my cheek to the back of my neck in one smooth motion. And then it went from my neck to my lower back so swiftly. His hands pressed into my skin so softly, sending a vibration through my body that caused me to lift off the heels of my feet onto the tip of my toes, while I wrapped my arms around his neck. I pulled back just to make sure this was not a dream. Opening my eyes, I saw Isaac in front of me and smiled.

"Are you okay?" he asked in a calm voice.

Smiling up at him, I grabbed the back of his neck, gently pulled him back into me, and kissed him again. Our lips moved equally together. Every kiss we shared in that moment was absolutely incredible. For the rest of the day, we sat and talked to each other about everything. As the sun began to go down, Isaac walked me to my car. He kissed me softly on the lips before we said good-bye.

Driving home, I felt so lucky to have found Isaac. He truly was amazing. Walking into my room, I fell across my bed. Laying there staring up at the ceiling, I couldn't help but think about that special moment that I shared with Isaac earlier today. Never had I been so consumed by someone before. Everything about him made me ache for him even more. At that moment as I sat up in my bed, I realized and knew now that I was deeply and uncontrollably in love with him.

Reaching for my phone on the nightstand, I noticed it wasn't there. Looking around the room, I noticed it on my desk. I really didn't feel like getting up to get it.

"I wish it was over here by me," I said to myself.

The phone then lifted up off my desk and floated into my hand.

"What the hell?" I said to myself.

I then heard a ladder come up against my window. It was Kyle coming up on the side of my house.

Looking in shock, I threw my phone out of my hand. I walked over to the window to help Kyle climb through. "Here let me help you."

"I got it," he said.

Still looking very much in shock, I began to talk to Kyle. "So what brings you here?" I sat back on my bed.

He walked from the window to my bed and sat at the edge. "I wanted to come and apologize again for being a jerk and not being there for you."

Still in shock, I continued to stare into space in denial. Feeling a slight tug on my shoulder, I came out of my shocked state.

"What? I'm sorry. What did you say?"

"Are you okay?" he asked.

"Yeah, I'm just a little tired. But what were you saying?"

"I know I haven't been a good friend to you lately, and I'm sorry for that. Even so, you have to admit that night was very strange. And I'm sorry, but I panicked. I literally thought you were possessed or something."

"Do you remember anything from that night?"

"That's the funny thing. I remember everything. The pain. The noises. I even felt my body lifting into the air. I could also hear you yelling for me. However, for some reason, I couldn't wake up. I mean, I tried everything, but I would not budge." My eyes filled with discomfort as I continued talking to Kyle. "I remember that, when I woke up, my eyes felt like they were on fire, and I also noticed this." I lifted up my left arm to show Kyle the symbol on my inner wrist.

"What the hell?" he responded.

I quickly locked my eyes on Kyle, and I was a little insulted.

"I'm sorry. This is all a little weird."

"You think?" I said in a very irritated tone.

"Look, I understand if you don't want to be my friend anymore. I get it."

"Wait, why would you think I wouldn't want to be your friend anymore?" he asked. "Look." He grabbed my hands. "I am your best friend. I have always been there for you. We have constantly been there for each other. And that's not going to change. Not now. Not ever. Hey, look at me," he said softly.

I lifted my head to be equal with his. I noticed a very comforting look into his eyes.

"We will figure this out together." He reached up to move away a strand of hair from my face with his index finger and slid it behind my ear.

A tiny smile appeared on my face. "Okay."

"Even so, before we get to that." He paused as he walked over to the desk chair where his bag was hanging on my chair. He reached carefully in his bag and pulled out a silver box with a lavender bow tied around it. Walking back over to me, he sat next to me on my bed. "This is for you." He carefully handed the box to me, placing it in my hands.

Kyle was always full of surprises. That was actually one of the things I loved about him. Carefully untying the ribbon, I opened the top of the box. I could not help but smile at what I saw inside. It was a vanilla cupcake with white frosting. I took the cupcake out of the box and placed it in my hand.

"This is great, Kyle. Thank you so much."

He positioned himself on my bed so he was fully facing me. "Everyone should celebrate her birthday." Reaching into his pocket, he took out a candle and a box of matches. He topped the cupcake with the candle and lit it. "Now, close your eyes and make a wish."

Continuing to smile, I closed my eyes and sat there for a second. Opening my eyes, I took in a short breath and blew out the candle. Kyle took his finger to scoop up some icing and wiped it across the tip of my nose.

"Hey, that wasn't very nice."

"Okay, you're right. Here, let me wipe it off." Kyle wiped the icing off my nose very gently with his finger.

"Thanks," I said to him with a gentle smile.

"I have one more gift to give you."

"Kyle, you didn't have to get me anything else. Really, you have done enough."

"No, I have to give this gift to you now, or I might not give it to you at all."

"Okay." I had a very curious look on my face.

"Just close your eyes."

"Do I really have to?"

"Please, just close your eyes." He grabbed my hand.

Closing my eyes, I just sat and waited. He was making sure to move very slowly. He moved into me until he was face-to-face with me.

"Kyle," I said just to make sure he was still there.

At the same time, I did not hear an answer. Then suddenly, I felt the warmth of his lips on mine. *Am I really letting this happen?* I thought to myself as his lips moved with mine.

He then slowly pulled away. I opened my eyes, not really believing what just happened.

"Happy birthday, Nichole," he whispered to me.

I opened my mouth to say something, but he put his finger over my mouth. "Don't say anything." He got up off the bed.

Grabbing his bag off the chair, he walked over to the window. As he stepped onto the ladder, he stopped to look at me. Looking back at him, I was in shock at what just happened.

"Good night." He then he climbed down the ladder and went home.

"What the hell just happened?" I said to myself. "Kyle just kissed me, and I didn't even pull back or try to stop him. How could I have let that happen?"

Falling back onto my bed, I laid there wondering to myself what to do about Kyle. *I should just keep my distance. I can't do that. He is my best friend. I just have to let him know that we cannot let it happen again and I don't see him that way. I mean, I can't see him that way. I'm with Isaac. At least, I think I am.*

My cell phone started to ring on the floor. I walked over and picked my phone up off the floor. I looked at the caller ID, and it was Isaac. A panicked feeling came over my body. *Do I tell him what just happened? No, I'll tell him later, not now. No, I have to tell him. Just answer the phone.*

"Hello," I said in a very calm voice.

"Hey, I didn't catch you at a bad time, did I?"

"Of course not," I said.

It couldn't be an even crazier time, I thought to myself.

"Well, I called you to see what you are doing tomorrow."

"I will have nothing to do tomorrow. And even if I did, I would clear my whole schedule just to see you."

"Wow, that's perfect. So why don't you meet me at the river tomorrow? Let's say at three in the afternoon."

"It sounds perfect to me," I replied.

"Okay, I will see you there."

"All right," I said with excitement.

"Nichole?"

"Yeah?" I replied.

"Good night."

Hearing him say that to me made me feel so peaceful. I couldn't help but smile. "Good night. Bye."

"Bye."

Lowering the phone from my ear, I knew I had to tell Isaac tomorrow about me and Kyle's kissing. *It's the right thing to do. Isaac is too important to me to lose.*

CHAPTER 12

The next morning, I rolled over on my back in my bed and faced the ceiling. I couldn't help but think about yesterday. *I have to be honest with the both of them and tell them the truth about how I feel. I have my best friend whose friendship means the world to me, and I don't want to lose that. Nevertheless, I have to tell him that we are just friends and that's all we will ever be.*

I grabbed my pillow, put it over my face, and let out a loud scream of frustration. Lifting the pillow from my face, I sat up in my bed and let out a big sigh. *Today is going to be a good day. I know it. I hope.*

Later that afternoon, I began getting ready for my day with Isaac. *What should I wear?*

I tried on so many things. Then finally in the back of my closet was a knit skater dress. It fit me perfectly. A little above my knees, it flared out so smoothly. It was sleeveless and had a double scoop neck and zipped up in the back.

"This is perfect," I said to myself.

To make it all come together, I put on my studded denim jacket with my cowboy boots that came up to my calves. My hair dangling with loose curls finished my look. I was ready to go see Isaac. I could not wait to be standing in front of him.

The drive over to the river could not have gone any quicker. All I wanted to do was see him. Pulling up to the field in my car, I could see Isaac facing the mountains. He looked so peaceful and content. Parking the car, I took a deep breath and got out of the car.

Walking up to him, I could see a path of Multiflora roses leading to a picnic formed on a silk sheet on the ground. The closer I got to him, the more I could feel my knees weakening with every step I took.

As he heard me getting closer, he turned around with the most welcoming smile on his face. I couldn't resist but smile back. He held out his hand for me to grab as an invitation to the picnic. I grabbed his hand, and he pulled me in close to hug me.

"This is so sweet," I said to him.

"This is for you. I just thought that, since you didn't get the chance to celebrate your birthday, we could celebrate it together. A belated birthday picnic. And after you told me everything that you have been going through, I just thought I could do something nice for you to get your mind off everything and enjoy the day."

"It's perfect."

Sitting there on the blanket, I noticed there was nothing but fruits and desserts spread all over. Any fruit or dessert you could think of was in front of me. There were also white rose petals everywhere even on the ground, spread around.

"Thank you so much for all of this."

"You're welcome." He smiled.

We sat there enjoying the picnic and each other's company for hours. Everything was perfect. Being lost in the moment, I noticed the sun going down.

"Wow, what time is it?" Looking on my phone, I noticed that the time was eight o'clock. "I should get going."

"Okay, how about I pack everything up and follow you back to your house?"

"It sounds great," I said.

I was really happy with his decision. I wasn't quite ready to say good-bye just yet. Pulling up in front of my house, we both got out of our cars and met each other in front of the porch steps.

"I had an amazing time. Thank you so much for what you did for me today."

We both walked up the steps to the front door.

"You're welcome," he said to me as we both turned and faced each other.

"Today was . . ."

Before I could finish my sentence, Isaac connected our lips together in a passionate kiss. He pulled me in closer to him, closing the gap between us. He then wrapped his arm around my lower back and placed his free hand gently on my cheek. I slowly placed my hand over his hand on my cheek. I was lost in this moment of passion. I slowly pulled away for a second to look into his eyes.

"What's wrong?" he asked in a very soft voice.

Pausing for a second to get the courage to say what I needed him to hear, I gently put his cheek in the palm of my hand. Letting out a deep breath, I slowly allowed the three words to flow out of my mouth.

"I love you."

It was quiet for a split second. Then a look of relief appeared on his face, along with a smile. He leaned in close to me for our noses to touch. Then he allowed the same words plus one to leave his mouth.

"I love you too," he said to me as our lips connected together.

While pulling myself to him even tighter, he lifted me up off my feet while continuing to kiss me. This moment was perfect. I didn't ever want it to end.

Placing me back down to my feet, he slowly removed his lips from mine.

"I should go inside."

"Yeah, you're right. So I'll see you tomorrow." He wrapped his arms around my waist.

"Yes, of course you will," I told him.

Grabbing his face and pulling him into me, I kissed his warm, soft lips one last time before walking to the front door. Forcing myself to walk through the front door, I stopped to turn around in the doorway. "Isaac."

He stopped on the steps and turned around to face me.

"Good night," I said to him.

"Good night," he replied.

Closing the door was so hard for me to do. I missed him already. I could not wait until I saw him tomorrow. Leaning up against the door, I learned my head back and closed my eyes.

I stood there in a daze and slid my fingers across my lips, thinking about how his fit so perfectly against mine. Then I slid my hand from my cheek to the side of my neck, reminiscing over from when his hands were once there. I opened my eyes, and a smile grew on the side of my mouth. Pushing up off the door, I walked toward the stairs.

"Nichole, is that you?"

Turning my attention to the living room, I saw Kristen sitting on the couch reading a book. With her back facing me, I walked into the living room to greet her.

"Yeah, it's me."

"Did you have a good time with Chelsea and Amy today?" she asked.

"Actually, I didn't hang out with them today." Sitting down next to her, I looked at her with the biggest smile on my face.

Sitting there looking at me, she put her hand on my cheek. "Wow, I haven't seen you smile like that since you were a little girl." Lowering her hand from my face to rest it on her leg, she widened her eyes in excitement. "Is this about a guy?"

I couldn't hold back my excitement as I answered her. "Yes, he's great too. He's sweet, charming, and so polite, and he's a perfect gentleman. You would really like him."

"I bet I would. He sounds dreamy." She leaned into me.

Looking down at my hands in my lap, I took a small sigh up under my breath.

"What's wrong, sweetie?"

I lifted my head up so I was at eye level with her. "It's just that we haven't talked like this in a long time. I don't know. I guess I miss our talks. That's all."

Putting my hand into hers, she smiled at me with the warmest look on her face. "So do I."

"Thank you for always being there for me. I don't thank you two enough, and I should. You and Uncle Matthew have given up so much just to make sure I have everything."

"And we would do it all over again. Nichole, I know we didn't do anything for you on your birthday, but your uncle and I did get you a gift. We just didn't know when to give it to you with everything that's been going on lately."

"It's fine. Trust me. I really didn't feel like celebrating anyway. Nevertheless, you and Uncle Matthew can give me my gift whenever you want."

"Okay, well how about this? Why don't you meet your uncle and me outside tomorrow morning and we will give you your gift then? I really want him to see your face when you see your gift."

"Okay, sounds great to me." Smiling back at her, I stood to my feet. "Good night."

"Good night, sweetheart," she replied back.

Walking upstairs and into my room, I got ready for bed. Climbing into my bed, I wrapped myself comfortably in my blanket. I reached over and turned off the light on my nightstand. I laid my head back onto my pillow and closed my eyes as I drifted off to sleep.

Later that night while sound asleep in my bed, I heard someone calling my name. The voice was very strong and firm. I slowly opened my eyes to see a bright light coming from my wall in my room. Lifting myself to sit up in my bed, the voice continued to call me over to it.

Stepping onto the hardwood floor in my room, the floor felt warm. A very soft breeze lifted my hair behind me so softly, making it flow through the air. When I reached the light, a body began to form right in front of me. It was a man in light blue clothing with dark blue outlining whose face was very welcoming. The color of his eyes was so similar to mine.

"Hello, Nichole," he said to me. "You have grown into a beautiful young woman. You are the spitting image of your mother."

"What? How do you know my name?"

"I don't have much time. I only have a few minutes before I have to go."

"What? Go where?"

"Nichole, listen to me. You are in extreme danger. Someone is after you. I don't know how he found you, but he did. You must not trust anyone. For what looks and feels safe to you will only bring you danger."

He took one step toward me and turned me around so I was facing the mirror in my room. He placed a necklace with a blue crystal tied on a clear string around my neck.

"I have seen this crystal before. I've dreamed about it."

"You are very special, Nichole. Your birth and destiny has been written among the stars."

As I looked into the mirror, I noticed my eyes and the symbol on my left inner wrist turning blue as the crystal began to glow. "What is happening to me?"

"You are becoming one with your true self."

I turned back around to face him. "And what is that?"

Lifting his arm, he showed me the same symbol on his inner left wrist. Lifting up my arm, I looked at the same symbol on my inner left wrist.

"You have one too."

"What does this mean?" I looked at my wrist.

Smiling at me, he took a step back into the light. "You and the crystal are connected now. Never take it off. Keep it next to you always."

"What does this all mean? Who are you?"

"I'm out of time. Remember what I told you. Good-bye, Nichole."

"Wait, please. You have to tell me what this all means."

And within a second, he was gone. Looking confused of what just happened, I turned on the light in my room and walked back over to the mirror. My eyes went back to their normal color. And my symbol and the crystal were no longer glowing.

I walked over to my bed. Slowly lying down, I wrapped myself back into my blanket and rested my head on my pillow. Turning over to look up at my ceiling, I was trying so hard to wrap my head around to what just happen. *Who was he? What did he mean about not trusting anyone I am comfortable with? What does this symbol mean?* I had so many questions with no answers.

Closing my eyes, I took a deep breath and exhaled. My phone rang on my nightstand. I reached over to grab it and wondered who could be calling me.

"Hello," I answered in the softest tone.

"Hi, I didn't wake you, did I?"

Smiling into the phone, I noticed the very calm sound of Isaac's voice on the other end of the phone. "No, of course not. I'm just laying here in bed. Is everything okay?"

"Yes! Of course it is," he answered. "I just wanted to call and say thank you for today. I had a really great time."

"No, thank you. You made me feel so special today. It's like you knew exactly what I needed. You are just amazing," I said to him.

"Well, I wouldn't say I'm amazing."

"You know you're right. I would say you're perfect."

There was a short pause on the phone. "Do you want to ride to school with me tomorrow?"

"I would love to. However, I have to take Amy to school tomorrow. Why don't we meet in the school parking lot?"

"It sounds great," he said.

"So I guess this means that we are official."

"Nichole, we were official when our lips connected together the first time we kissed. So I will see you tomorrow?"

"Yes, I will be there waiting for you, beautiful."

"Okay, good night, Isaac."

"Good night. I hope your dreams are as beautiful as you are."

"Thank you."

"You're welcome."

"Bye. Bye."

CHAPTER 13

After waking up the next morning, excitement filled me. Not only was I going to see Isaac today, but I was also going to receive my gift from my aunt and uncle this morning. Getting up out of bed, I rushed into my bathroom to get washed up for school. After finishing up in my bathroom, I got dressed and headed downstairs for breakfast.

Walking into the kitchen, I noticed no one was cooking, and everything was put up. *That's weird. Oh, well. I will just stop and get a bite to eat on the way to school.*

I grabbed my bag and keys and headed out the front door. As the door closed behind me, I couldn't do anything but be amazed at what I was seeing. My aunt and uncle were both standing next to a black, brand-new, four-door Audi RS 7 sedan.

"Happy birthday, sweetheart," said Aunt Kristen.

Running down the steps, I grabbed and hugged them both. "Thank you so much."

"You are very welcome, sweetie. I think you will need this key to drive to school today." My uncle placed the key in my hand as I jumped up and down with excitement.

Unlocking my new car, I got in and closed the door. The inside of my car was all black with leather seats. Starting up the car, I rolled down the window and looked at Matthew and Kristen.

"Make sure not to drive fast. You have to get used to this car first, all right?"

"Okay, I promise." I pulled off and headed to Amy's house.

Riding in the car with Amy was very quiet. I could feel her eyes staring at me.

"Are you okay?" she asked.

"Yes, I'm fine."

"I can see that. You have this awesome new car, and you can't stop smiling."

"No, I'm just happy. That's all."

"Well, it's good to see you smiling again."

"Thanks, Amy."

"You're welcome."

Pulling into the school parking lot, I could see Isaac sitting on the hood of his car, waiting for me. Parking my car next to his, he walked over to my door to let me out.

"I see someone got a new car," he said to me.

"Yes, I just got it this morning. It was a birthday gift from my aunt and uncle."

Amy got out of the car with a very shocked look on her face. When I looked at her, I knew exactly what she was thinking. I smiled at her as Isaac closed my car door for me.

Walking to the front of my car, Amy just looked at Isaac.

"So you must be Amy." Isaac walked up to her to shake her hand. "Hi, I'm Isaac. It's nice to meet you."

Taking his hand to shake it, she gave him a friendly smile. "Nice to meet you too, and yes, I am Amy." Letting go of his hand, she gave him a very serious look. "Just to let you know, if you hurt her, I will kill you."

Smiling back at Amy, he simply said, "I will never hurt her. Hurting her would be like hurting myself."

"Well, good," Amy said.

"Okay, how about we head to class?" I said while walking up to them.

Walking up to the school together with his hand holding mine, I could see Chelsea looking confused and surprised at the same time. I really didn't care. I was happy, and that was all that mattered.

Amy grabbed her by the arm, and she began walking with us. As we walked into the double doors of the school, we walked right past Tyler. *I really hope he is happy.*

I stopped at my locker to get a book that I needed for my first class while Amy, Chelsea, and Isaac went to theirs. Standing there at my locker, I could see Kyle out of the corner of my eye, walking up to me.

"Hey, Nichole," he said in a very intimidating voice.

"Hey, Kyle," I replied back.

"So you and the new kid, huh?"

"Don't start, Kyle."

"What? I'm just saying it's a little soon, don't you think? I mean you don't even really know him, Nichole."

"No, you don't know him. For your information, he was there for me at the darkest time in my life, so back off. Look, I don't know what it is about him." I looked over at Isaac at his locker. "He consumes me in some way."

"Oh, really? He consumes you now."

Closing my locker, I rolled my eyes at Kyle and started to walk away from him.

"Okay, Nichole, wait."

"What, Kyle?"

"You know me. There is just something not right with this guy. He is hiding something. Just look at him."

Turning to look at Isaac, I smiled. He looked fine to me. Walking up in front of me, Isaac kissed me on the cheek.

"Hey, it's Kyle, right?"

"Yeah, and you are?"

"Isaac."

"Oh, yeah, the new kid no one knows anything about."

"Kyle." I looked very annoyed.

"What?"

"Well, we should get to class," said Isaac as he put his arm around me.

"Yeah, you should," Kyle said rudely.

"It was nice meeting you," replied Isaac.

"Yeah, wish I could say the same," said Kyle.

"You don't have to be so rude," I said to Kyle.

"It's fine. I'll just meet you after your class," Isaac said

"Okay, I'll see you later."

Looking back at Kyle, I couldn't be anything but furious with him. "What is wrong with you, Kyle?"

"I don't like him, Nichole. Something is not right about him."

"You know what? You don't have to like him. I'm with him, not you. I don't need your permission." Walking far from him, I stopped to turn and look at him. "Thanks for being a good friend." I then turned around and walked away.

"I'm just worried about you. Why can't you see that?" he yelled to me. He hit his locker with his hand and walked away.

Walking into my first class, I took my seat, just hoping today would go by quickly. A few minutes passed in class when my phone vibrated in my pocket. I took my phone out of my pocket to find a text from Isaac that read, "You are so beautiful."

Smiling at my phone, I texted back, "You are so silly, but I love that handsome face of yours."

First period went by really fast. At the end of the class, we were still sending text messages back and forth to each other. The bell rang, letting everyone know the class was over. Getting up from my seat, I grabbed my things and walked out of the classroom. And there was Isaac, waiting for me outside the door just like he had promised.

Taking his hand into mine, we both just smiled at each other. Walking to my next class, I looked up at Isaac and could tell something was bothering him.

"Hey, are you okay?" I asked.

Pulling me off to the side, he seemed worried. Making sure that my attention was on him, he took in a deep breath. "I don't think your friend Kyle likes me very much."

"So you could tell, huh?" I said with such sarcasm.

"Come on, Nichole."

"I'm just joking," I said. "I know Kyle will warm up to you."

"What if he doesn't? Then what? You'll choose between us?"

Looking very confused, I quickly let go of his hand. "What are you saying?"

"Look, I will never tell you to choose. Nevertheless, I know he is important to you. And all I am saying is this. Do you really want to have a boyfriend and a best friend who can't stand each other?"

Pulling me in gently to him, he kissed me on my lips so softly. "I just want you to be happy. And I know having the both of us in your life will make you happy. So whatever you want me to do to win him over, I will do it."

Looking up at him, I couldn't help but smile. I lifted up on my tiptoes and kissed him on the lips. Lowering back down to the soles of my feet, I rested my head on his chest and hugged him.

"Thank you."

When I was looking up at Isaac, he noticed the necklace around my neck.

"Where did you get this?" he asked with concern in his voice.

"It's actually a crazy story."

Before I could even tell him the story, he pulled away from me. "I should get to my next class."

"Are you okay?"

"Yeah, I'm fine," he said.

"I will meet you after."

"Okay." I let him go and watched him walk away in the opposite direction.

Sitting in second period, all I could think about was what Isaac said to me. Even so, he was right. *What if Kyle can't accept Isaac and me being together? Kyle's friendship is very important to me. However, I can't jeopardize what I have with Isaac. I won't.*

Second period seemed as if it would never end. Then finally the bell rang. Walking out of second period, Isaac was right there, waiting for me outside the door.

"So are you ready for lunch?"

"Yes, I really need a break from all that thinking. Hey! Are you okay? You looked off last period."

"Oh, yeah. I'm fine. I just didn't want to be late for second period."

Putting his arm around me, we both walked to the cafeteria. Walking into the lunchroom in the middle of the day was the break I needed. All that classwork was hurting my head.

"Are you hungry?" Isaac asked.

"Not really. I think I'm just going to have a fruit salad."

"Okay, you go sit at your table, and I will get it for you."

"Thank you."

"You're welcome."

I walked over to the table where Amy and Chelsea were sitting and took a seat at the table. They both were staring at me and smiling from ear to ear.

"Tell me all the details, and don't leave anything out," Chelsea said.

"What are you guys talking about?"

"Don't act like that. We can see it all over your face, Nichole," she said.

"Really." I smiled.

"Yes," said Amy excitedly.

"Not now. He will be back soon."

"Okay, but don't think you are off the hook."

While Isaac was walking to get in line for my fruit salad, Tyler purposefully bumped into him.

"Watch where you are going!" yelled Tyler.

"Sorry. My mistake," replied Isaac.

"Yeah, you're right it is your mistake."

Looking furious, Tyler walked up to Isaac, standing eye to eye with him. The entire lunchroom got very quiet. Turning around in my chair to see what was going on, I noticed Tyler and Isaac standing eye to eye with each other.

"Oh no." I got up from my chair and rushed over to them, forcing my way into the middle of the two of them. With a hand on each of their chests, I extended my arms to separate them.

"What the hell are you doing with my girl?" asked Tyler very angrily.

"I'm not your girl anymore, Tyler."

Looking at me, Tyler slapped my hand off his chest.

"Look, we don't want any trouble." Isaac put his arm in front of me and pulled me behind him.

Not liking what he saw, Tyler reached behind Isaac and roughly grabbed me by the arm. "Nichole, let's go. You're coming with me."

"Tyler, let me go." I snatched away my arm. Looking Tyler in his face, I took my other hand and slapped him. "Don't ever touch me again!"

Feeling rage going through his veins, he turned back to look at me. He lifted his hand and slapped me in the face, causing me to fall to the ground. Feeling nothing but rage, with full force, Isaac rushed over to Tyler and punched him in the face, making him fall to the floor. Reaching down to grab him, he threw him across the room onto a table, throwing him into other students as they all fell to the ground.

Walking over to me, Isaac knelt down to help me up off the ground. "Are you okay?" Putting my hurt cheek in his hand, he made sure to be as gentle as he possibly could.

"Yeah, I think so."

Surprised at what just happened, I stood up on my feet and lifted up my head to look him in his eyes. "Your eyes." I looked confused.

"What?" asked Isaac.

"Your eyes are blue."

Panicking, Isaac turned away from me and walked out of the lunchroom quickly.

"Isaac, wait!" I yelled at him.

Running after him into the hall, I continued calling after him, trying to catch him. Following him into the student parking lot, I saw him peeling off in his car. Lifting my hair from my face, I stood there in confusion. Then my eyes widened, and my mouth dropped open. In that moment, I realized that the man I loved was just like me.

CHAPTER 14

It'd been three weeks since the incident with Tyler, Isaac, and me. I'd left Isaac more than a hundred messages. I needed him to tell me what was going on, but he would not return any of my phone calls. I couldn't take this silence anymore between us. He owed me an explanation.

Then out of nowhere, a thought went through my mind of what the guy told me the one night in my room. He had to be just like me. His eyes turned blue like mine did. *Is he the one the guy was talking about? Is Isaac the one after me? I have to know the answers to these questions.*

Sitting at the dining room table, I noticed my aunt coming to sit next to me. "Hey, sweetie," she said with a warm and concerned look on her face.

"Hey," I replied to her.

"Still haven't heard from him, huh?"

Shaking my head no, I couldn't help but look down at my lap. "I am so angry at him. Nevertheless, I miss him so much." With tears flowing down my cheeks, I tried so hard to hold them back.

"Honey, look at me. There is not one guy on this earth worth your tears. If he wants to be a jerk, then that's on him. Trust me. He will realize what he has. That's if he hasn't already."

I smiled back at her as I lifted my head to look at her. *She has no idea the truth of why Isaac is not communicating with me anymore. And I can't tell her the truth. She will not be able to handle it, and she will think I'm a freak and Isaac too. So I will just tell her what she needs to hear.*

"Yeah, I guess you're right."

"That's true. I'm right. Now how about I fix us some ice cream, and we can eat until we pass out?"

"Sounds great," I said to her.

She patted me on the back while getting up from the table and went into the kitchen. Continuing to sit at the table and think to myself, my phone began to vibrate on the table. I really didn't feel like talking to anyone right now. Grabbing my phone, I noticed it was Isaac calling me. I felt my entire body begin to freeze up. Wiping the tears from my eyes, I cleared my throat and answered.

"Hello."

"Hey, Nichole. Before you say anything, I called you so you can meet me somewhere to talk."

"No, we can talk now, Isaac."

"Nichole, please. What I have to say is very important, and I'd rather say it in person instead of over the phone."

"Fine. Meet you were?"

"My house. I will text you the address."

"Okay, I'll be there shortly."

Hanging up the phone, I sat at the table waiting for the address. Aunt Kristen was making her way back into the dining room with two bowls of ice cream when I received the text from Isaac.

"Is it okay if we do this another time?"

"Why? Is something wrong?"

"No, I just got a text from Isaac, and he wants to talk."

Placing the two bowls of ice cream onto the table, she looked at me with a smile. "Sure, sweetie. You go do what you have to do. We can do this later tonight."

"Sounds like a plan," I said to her.

Getting up from the table, I grabbed my phone and headed upstairs to get dressed. Coming downstairs, I went into the dining room and hugged Aunt Kristen by surprise.

"What is this for?"

"Thank you for talking to me."

"Anytime. Just remember to drive safely and make him beg." She smiled.

Letting her go, I smiled back at her and headed out the door. The drive to Isaac's house was about twenty minutes long. Driving past nothing but open and empty fields, I could tell I was in the middle of nowhere. When I arrived at Isaac's house, I was so amazed at what I saw.

I turned off the long road onto an extended driveway that led to his house. The house was built in a French country style. It looked to be on over six acres of land. With all parts of the house covered in stone, its light gray color was really beautiful with large windows going all around the house.

Stepping out of my car, I just stood still for a moment. Taking in a deep breath, I walked up to the front double doors of his home. The build of them seemed to be very modern. I rang the doorbell, waiting for Isaac to answer the door. He must have been waiting right by the door because I only had to ring it once, and the door opened with him standing in the doorway.

"Hey," I said while standing in front of him.

"Hey, come in."

As I walked into his house, I saw a huge foyer with a table right in the middle. The ceilings were very high in his house. A beautiful wooden staircase going up to the second floor was very elegant to me.

"You have a very amazing home."

"Thank you."

"And you stay here by yourself?"

"Yes, I do."

"Wow, must be nice."

"No, not really. It gets very lonely at times. How about we go into the living room and talk?"

"Sure."

As I walked into the living room, I saw a couch placed right in front of the fireplace. The furniture in the house was very modern but beautiful. I sat down on the couch, and Isaac sat down a couple of inches from me on the same couch.

"Would you like something to drink?"

"Why haven't you answered any of my phone calls or called me back?"

"I guess you don't want anything to drink," he said, trying to break some of the tension in the room.

I gave him a very aggravated look as I tilted my head to the side slightly.

"Okay, fine. I'm sorry. Nevertheless, the truth is that I was afraid."

"Afraid of what?" I asked.

"That you would be afraid of me."

"Why would I be frightened of you?"

Standing up to his feet, he walked, stood in front of the fireplace, and turned to face me. "There is a lot that you don't know about me."

Standing up, I walked in front of him and planted my feet to the ground. "I have a lot about me that you don't know about too. Trust me."

"It's nothing like this."

Taking two steps up to him, I closed the distance between us. I looked up in his eyes and planted the palm of my hand on the side of his neck. "Whatever it is, we will both figure it out together. You can tell me."

Walking away from me, he stood over by the built-in bookshelf. "I didn't just come back here because I was homesick. I came back because of you."

"What do you mean?"

Lifting up his sleeve on his left arm, he took two steps closer to me, held out his arm to me, and turned his forearm so I could see the inside of his wrist. As I got closer, I saw the same symbol on his inner wrist. It was identical to the one I had on mine.

"Why do you have the same marking that I have?"

"Because, Nichole, we are from the same species."

"What are you talking about? What species?"

"The Agjavise."

"What the hell are you talking about, Isaac?" I backed up in fear.

"We are a powerful group that lives among humans in silence."

"Isaac, stop it. You're scaring me," I said to him.

"An evil destroyer called Valcuse destroyed our planet. He wanted to take over the planet and use it for his own selfish reasons. The only way he would do so was by collecting power from the twelve crystals from the twelve families that were connected to them. Each family had a firstborn that inherited the crystals, making it so the firstborn of each of the twelve families held the power of the crystals instead of the families.

"Making sure that Valcuse would never get the power he needed, the families put together a spell that made sure the children would not get their powers until the night of their eighteenth birthdays and would be marked with the Agjavise mark to remind them of where they came from and the importance of their birth.

"Out of the twelve families, one child would rise and lead the rest into battle as the savior to all. It is written that he or she will be faster, smarter, and stronger than all and bring light to the darkness of the people. To protect the children, the families transported from their planet to this one.

"The families had fake crystals made and the mothers of the families would wear one, so just in case Valcuse caught them, he wouldn't get the real thing. Most of the families except the children are dead. Valcuse followed them here and took out his wrath on them, killing everyone but five of the remaining family's adults.

"I have been searching for the firstborn, and I have only found five, including you and me. Nichole, I was not planning on staying in town this long. However, when I saw you for the first time, I just had to get to know you. I felt drawn to you for some reason. It was like this energy connected us. Somehow I feel stronger when I'm with you and weaker when I'm away from you."

Walking over to me, he stopped in front of me. "When you put your arms around me, I feel like I'm home in your arms."

Leaning in to kiss me, I punched him in the stomach and started to run. As I reached the foyer, Isaac appeared from nowhere in front of me.

Gasping for air, I was frozen in disbelief. "How did you do that?"

"Don't be afraid of me, please. You are the same as me. Nichole, it is said that the savior will be the one who will need the most convincing. And he or she will be the last born of the twelve. You are the last born of the twelve. You are the one who will bring light to darkness."

"Why are you telling me all of this?" I asked.

"You once asked me why you felt so drawn to me. And I told you that you would know when you're ready. I'm telling you the truth now because you are ready now."

"You said that I was the last born. How old are you?"

"I am twenty-four. I was the sixth born. Before my parents died, they told me that I was destined to fall in love with the one born of prophecy." Walking up to me, he lifted my chin with his hand so I could meet his eyes. "I will help you through this. You are the reason I have a life now. I live for you, Nichole." Touching my nose with his, he pulled me in close to him. "Do you trust me?"

"Yes," I said very softly.

He connected our lips like never before. The power and energy flowed through our bodies, making it feel like I was floating. I closed my eyes and gripped his lips tighter with mine, making it impossible to separate from one another.

Lowering back down to my feet away from his lips, I kept my eyes closed. "This is impossible right?"

Opening my eyes, I looked up at him with confusion and noticed a small smile appear on his face.

"Nothing is impossible."

"So what all can I do then?" I asked.

Turning my back into him, he softly whispered into my ear, "Close your eyes and think of a place you can see yourself right know."

Closing my eyes, I could see myself standing in the middle of an open, grassy field. I then felt a strong breeze flowing through my hair. I felt my legs getting goose bumps from the wind. I thought of the field being surrounded by tall trees, and on one of them was a tire swing hanging from a tree branch. I could smell the greenery of the field.

"Okay, now open your eyes," Isaac whispered to me.

I opened my eyes, and I was standing in the middle of the field. Looking at my left, I could see Isaac standing next to the tire swing smiling at me. As I continued standing in that same spot, I focused my attention on Isaac, wanting to be standing by the tree with him. Within a blink of an eye, I was in his arms by the tree.

"How is this even possible? I mean, this is just incredible."

"Yes, it is, and so are you."

Looking up at him, I smiled at him and connected our lips. Pulling away, I remembered why I transported us here. My uncle and I used to come here all the time when I was little. He used to push me on this tire swing all the time. However, most of the time, we would play tag for hours out here. When we both would get tired, we would lie on the grass and look up at the clouds. We would tell each other what shape or object we thought the cloud looked like. I remember lying on my back and thinking to myself if there were anything beyond the clouds or if it just ended with them. *Well, now you know it doesn't end with them.*

Leaning into him, I looked at him with a comforting look in my eyes. "Kiss me."

"Whatever you want, you shall have," he said in a very soft voice. Our lips connected as we kissed passionately.

"Wow," I said while pulling back.

"Did you feel that?"

"Yes, that is our power flowing through our bodies. For our kind, when you fine your other half its like the urge to have or even kiss that person is unbearable. We are meant to be together. I mean we are soul mates after all."

Leaning back in, I connected our lips for another kiss. However, this kiss was different. It was more sexual and desirable. Moving his hand from my hip to my upper back under my shirt, I pulled away to catch my breath.

"So does this mean that we should make this official?" I smiled.

"Wow, you just go right to the point, don't you? I think we should wait until the right moment."

"And what is the right moment?"

"Trust me. We will both know."

Smiling, I pressed my lips onto his very passionately again.

"You know you make it very difficult for me to control myself when you kiss me like that."

"You know where I want to be right now?" I asked him.

He grabbed me by the hips very softly, and we disappeared and reappeared into his room. "This is exactly where I want to be."

Looking around his room, I was very surprised how modern it and the furniture were. He had a huge bed in the middle of his room. In the corner of his room, he had a desk with paintings laid out.

Walking over to his desk, I looked at the beautiful paintings, and I was amazed. "These are amazing. Did you paint these?"

"Yes, it's just something I do in my spare time. Nothing special though."

"Are you kidding? These are really good."

He walked to the side of his desk and looked at a painting on the wall in his room.

"It's beautiful," I said to him while walking to his side to admire the painting.

"Thank you."

The painting was of a woman's face. She had blue eyes, and her hair was covering every part of her face except for her eyes.

"I used to have this dream about a woman whose face I could never see. The only thing I would be able to see was her eyes. I was never afraid of her. I just knew that one day those beautiful eyes would lead me to the perfect face that they belonged to. So I painted this as a reminder to never stop searching for her. To have faith that I would find those eyes one day." Turning around to face me, he looked me straight in my eyes. "The first time I saw you in the hallway when we bumped into each other and our eyes met for the first time, the first thing that came to mind was my painting. I knew I had finally found the woman from my dream."

Taking his hand into mine, I walked over to his bed and kissed him.

"Trust me. As much as I want to do this, we should wait," he said to me while breathing heavily under his breath.

"Nevertheless, I need you now." I pushed him onto the bed, crawled on top of him, and started kissing him.

"Wait. Let's just slow down," he said.

"Hold on. Are you a virgin?" I asked.

"Of course I am. I really haven't had any time to do that with anyone," Isaac said sarcastically. "Wait. You're not?"

"No, I am. I just thought you would have plenty of girls throwing themselves at you. I mean, look at you. You're beautiful."

"Even though that might be true, I have no interest in other girls. All I want is you." He reached up to kiss me on my lips. "You are the one I want to become one with. And since both of us haven't experienced that yet, I want it to be special."

"So do I." Leaning back down to kiss him, my phone rang in my back pocket.

"Don't answer it." Isaac pleaded with me.

Getting my phone, I noticed it was Amy. "I have to. It's Amy."

"Hello," I answered.

"Hey, girl, are you okay? No one has heard from you in a while."

"Yes, I'm fine. I just needed to clear my head."

"About who?" Amy asked.

"No one. What's up?"

"Well, Alex from the cheer squad is throwing a party and wants us to come. So what time should Chelsea and I be ready?"

Looking back at Isaac on the bed, I paused for a second. "Let me call you back." Putting the phone down, I continued to look at Isaac. "Amy and Chelsea want me to go to a party with them. I really haven't been spending time with them lately."

"You should go," said Isaac.

"You think?"

"Yeah, I can share you for one night."

Turning around to sit on my knees, I leaned into him with a very flirty movement from my body and leaned him back onto the bed. "No, I want to stay here with you."

Smiling back at me, he gave me a quick kiss on my lips. "Go have fun. Just remember you know everything about yourself now. Try to control yourself. You don't have control over your powers yet. And I haven't shown you everything that you can do yet."

"I promise I will be careful."

"Okay," he said.

"I will see you tomorrow," I said to him.

Pulling me into him, he planted his lips onto mine. Opening my mouth, I invited in his tongue to meet mine. As our lips separated, he gently bit my bottom lip before letting my lips go. "You know you're making it very difficult for me to leave."

"I'm sorry. I just love you so much, and I want you to know that every time I kiss you," he told me.

"Trust me. I know. And I love you for that." I gave him a quick kiss on the lips and got out of his bed.

"So I will see you tomorrow."

"Yes, you will," I told him.

"Okay, bye."

"Bye."

Walking out of the door and getting into my car, I turned around to look at him. "I miss you already." I got into my car and drove away.

I stopped at a nearby gas station to get some gas and decided to call Amy back. She had to be waiting by the phone because she answered on the first ring.

"So are you going?" she asked.

"Well, hello to you too, and yes, I'm just getting some gas right now."

"That's great. Okay, so how long before you get to my house?"

"I would say about fifteen minutes, so call Chelsea and let her know to be ready."

"Okay, I will see you when you get here."

"All right. Bye."

"Bye."

I finished putting gas into my car, got in, and drove away.

CHAPTER 15

Driving to Amy's house, I thought about Kyle. I hadn't talked to him in a while. I felt like I had really lost his friendship. I hated that he couldn't be happy for me. I really should call him. But what would I say? We really hadn't even talked about that kiss we shared. I hadn't even told Isaac about that kiss yet.

I really missed my best friend. I hoped he was okay. Pulling up into Amy's driveway, I put the car in park. Sitting there in the driver's seat, I just thought to myself about all the things I had been through in this short time of my senior year in high school: finding out my aunt and uncle were not really related to me, having Kyle kiss me, figuring out my destiny in life, and learning the fact I had so much power and abilities inside of me. However, most importantly, it was falling in love with Isaac. He really had made my life so much better in so many different ways.

While I was sitting in the car thinking, Amy must have seen me pull up because she ran up to the car and tapped on the window. Bringing me back to what was going on in the present, I looked right at her.

"What are you doing just sitting out here?"

"Just thinking," I said while opening the door.

"Oh, really about who?"

I gave her a very distinct look. Instantly, she knew who.

"How sweet," she said.

"Don't get out of the car. I'm ready, so let's just go get Chelsea, and we can head to the party."

"Okay."

Amy got into the car and called Chelsea to let her know that we were on our way and to be ready. When we pulled up in front of her house, she was already standing outside, prepared to jump in the car.

"This is what I'm talking about." She jumped into the car. "Girls' night out!" Chelsea screamed with excitement in her voice as I drove to Alex's house.

While I was pulling up to Alex's house, it was hard to find somewhere to park my car when we got there. Cars were everywhere: on the lawn, in the driveway, at the side of the house and streets, and even in a next door neighbor's yard. I decided to park my car around the corner. I wanted to make sure we would not be crammed in when we were ready to leave.

The party was bigger than I thought it was going to be. It seemed like the entire senior class was here. Walking through the front door, the way everyone's eyes turned on us, it seemed like everyone was waiting on us to get there.

Walking through the crowd, I turned my attention to the stairs. Staring at me with a small smile was Kyle. I thought he didn't come to these sorts of things. I rolled my eyes and continued to head to the kitchen to pour myself a drink. Carrying my drink in my hand, I went over to the living room where everyone was dancing. I stood in the door frame and watched Chelsea and Amy dance with each other. They looked like they were having so much fun.

"So Isaac allowed you to come out tonight?" I heard a voice say behind me.

Turning my head slightly, I realized Kyle was standing behind me. "What do you want, Kyle?"

"Look, I just know that, if you were with me, you wouldn't be here by yourself."

"I'm not here by myself."

"You know what I mean, Nichole."

"Yeah, well, it's just girls' night out."

"Well, I don't see you dancing with your girls."

"I don't feel like dancing."

Pausing for a quick moment, he sighed up under his breath. "I miss you, okay. I miss my best friend. Don't try to pretend that you don't miss me either."

I smiled as I turned to face him. "I do miss you, you idiot. Nevertheless, you have to accept that I'm with Isaac now, and that's not going to change."

"Even so, what about us? Nichole." He pleaded as he grabbed my hand into his.

"You are my best friend, Kyle, and that kiss should have never happened. Please, I just need you to be my friend."

"Okay, fine," he said with irritation in his voice.

"Nevertheless, can you at least dance with your friend?"

"Sure." I took a drink from my cup and put it on the table next to me. I grabbed his hand and led him to the dance floor.

Standing in the middle of the dance floor, we moved to the music. Moving my hips to the beat, Kyle looked down at them and placed his hands on my hips. I grabbed his hands and lifted them in the air with mine. As we lowered our hands back down to our side, Kyle pulled me in close to him and smiled at me. Not even knowing what would happen next, he smiled at me and then kissed me. I pushed him away from me and slapped him in the face. Running out the door, I could hear him calling me to stop.

Amy and Chelsea were watching everything and ran after me.

Chelsea grabbed Kyle and told him to back off. "Can't you see that you're just continuing to keep hurting her?"

Amy and Chelsea caught up to me, and we all got into the car and drove off. I dropped off Chelsea and Amy at their houses before driving to mine.

Pulling up in the driveway, I noticed Isaac sitting on the porch steps waiting for me. "Hey."

I got out of the car and walked up to him.

"Hey, did you have a good time?"

"For the most part, yes, I did."

"What are you doing here?"

"I just thought I would surprise you, and I wanted to tell you good night in person. I also met your Aunt Kristen. I think she really likes me. I was actually invited to an early dinner at your house Friday night before the football game."

"That's so sweet," I said while still having a guilty look on my face.

"What's wrong?" Isaac asked.

I paused with so much guilt in my eyes as I looked him in his. "I need to tell you something, but don't get upset, okay?"

With a very concerned look on his face, he agreed.

"Do you remember the day at the field when we shared our first kiss?"

"Yes, what about it?"

"Well, when I got home that night, Kyle stopped by to give me a gift for my birthday. He gave me a cupcake and told me that he had one more thing to give me. He asked me if I would close my eyes, so I did. And then he kissed me."

Backing up from me, he looked at me with great disappointment in his eyes. "Did you push him away?"

"It meant nothing to me."

"Did you push him away?"

"No. However, it meant nothing to me. He even kissed me again tonight."

"Wait, you kissed him once again?"

"No, he came on to me. Even so, I did push him away, and I slapped him." I saw Isaac's eyes begin to turn blue as he walked away. "Isaac, don't." I grabbed his arm.

"Nichole, let me go."

"No, we need to talk about this," I said.

"Let me go." As he turned around, he yanked his arm away from me.

Not realizing the force he was using, he threw me into the door, knocking me to the floor.

"Oh, Nichole," I heard him say. "I am so sorry."

I looked up to him. I noticed his eyes changing back to their normal color as he was calming down.

"It's okay," I told him.

"No, it's not. I'm so sorry," he told me.

And within a second, he was gone.

CHAPTER 16

The next morning, I got up to get ready for school. I didn't really feel like dressing up, so I just put on a T-shirt with some jeans.

Arriving at school that morning was very stressful. I hadn't talked to Isaac all night since our incident. And I really wanted to make things right between us. I missed him so much. My heart was aching for him. Walking into the hallway, I went to my locker to get my book for class. Putting my backpack in my locker, I grabbed the book that I needed.

Closing the locker door, Isaac was standing right there behind it.

"Hey," he said to me.

"Hey." I leaned into my locker.

Handing me a white rose from behind his back, he smiled at me. "This is for you."

"Thank you." I took the rose while smiling.

He gently pulled me close to him. "I am so sorry for last night. I should have never lost my temper like that."

"No, it was my fault. I should have told you about what happened instead of keeping it from you."

"That still does not excuse my behavior. I am so sorry, and I will never hurt you like that again." He touched his forehead to mine and then connected our lips as we kissed. Pulling away, he whispered in my ear, "I'm so sorry."

Looking out the corner of his eye, he saw Kyle standing at his locker. "I'll be right back." He gently pulled away from me.

"Isaac." I grabbed his arm.

He turned to look at me with the calmest eyes. "It's okay. I'm just going to talk to him. That's all."

He took me by the hand so I would walk over to Kyle's locker with him. Isaac tapped Kyle on the shoulder.

"What do you want?" Kyle turned around.

"I just wanted to say that I respect your friendship with Nichole, and I'm asking you to do the same with me and Nichole's relationship."

"Look, I'm never going to respect this thing you call a relationship. She belongs with me, not you. And trust me. I won't have to force her to kiss me again. 'Cause next time she will be willing to kiss me."

"Guys, stop it." I pulled Isaac away from Kyle.

Isaac pretended to walk away and then turned around and punched Kyle in the face, knocking him to the ground.

"Isaac, what is wrong with you?" I asked him in an angry voice. I knelt down to see if Kyle were okay and then looked back up to Isaac. He looked at me and walked away.

"Isaac, wait!" I looked back at Kyle with complete anger. "Are you happy now? Don't ever talk to me again."

I grabbed my book and went to class. The time could not go by any slower for the rest of the day at school. And when school was over for the day, I drove to Isaac's house to see if he were okay. Getting out of my car at Isaac's house was a little difficult. *I hope he doesn't think that I am upset with him.*

I reached the front of his house to ring the doorbell. A couple seconds had passed when he opened the door. Standing there in the door frame, he just stood there, not saying anything to me.

"Can I come in?" I asked, not being able to bear the silence between us.

"Sure." He stepped to the side.

"I am so sorry for what happened at school today," I said to him as he closed the door behind me.

Walking up to me, he placed his finger to my mouth, stopping me from finishing my sentence. "It's okay. I'm not upset with you. I felt myself getting angry, so I knew I needed to go somewhere and calm down before I did something that I would regret. So I left school and came home." He kissed me on the forehead. Taking my hand into his, he led me into the living room. "I want to show you something. Stand right here in the middle of the floor."

"Okay," I said with a curious tone in my voice.

Isaac walked behind me and put one arm around my waist and the other to use his hand to move my hair to one shoulder. He leaned into me to whisper into my ear. I could feel every nerve in my body all at once begin to tense up with the soft and warmth of his lips on my ear.

"Are your eyes closed?"

"Yes," I said in a very calm voice.

All of a sudden, I could feel a very cool breeze on my skin. I could feel the warmth from the sun and hear water crashing so gently up against something.

"Open your eyes," he whispered to me.

Opening my eyes, I was so amazed at the sight in front of me. The sun was setting on the water. The water was so calm, and the sky was so clear. I looked down to see the waves gently rushing up against the rocks below me. I stood there with Isaac behind me. I then realized that this was the same cliff where I wanted to end my life at one time.

"Is this the—"

"Yes," he said, cutting me off.

I looked very confused, not sure why he would think to transport us here. "Don't get me wrong. The view is so beautiful, but why bring me here?"

"You may have tried to end your life here at one time. Nevertheless, when I saved you that day, that's when my life started." He paused for a quick second. "My life started with you." Turning around to face me, he wrapped his arms around my waist. "You are everything to me, Nichole. I would do anything for you." Taking my cheek into his hand, he rubbed my cheek gently.

"Promise me that you will never leave me. That we will always be together," I said to him.

"I promise," he replied.

I pulled him into me and kissed him with more passion then I had ever before. While kissing him standing there on that cliff, I realized how blessed I was. The love I had once dreamed of was right in front of me. I definitely found my soul mate.

We stood there and watched the sun go down before leaving. He transported us back to his house and then drove my car back to my house, just so we could spend more time together.

Getting out of my car at my house, we both noticed that Kyle was sitting on the porch steps. We both walked and stood at the bottom of the steps, staring at Kyle.

"Hey, guys," Kyle said.

"Hey," I said back.

Isaac put his arm around my waist in a very protective way and pulled me close to him.

"Isaac, is it okay if I talk to Nichole in private?"

I looked up at Isaac and nodded my head, letting him know that everything was okay.

"Sure." Isaac kissed me on the lips and smiled at me. "I will just see you tomorrow."

"Okay."

He gave Kyle a quick look and walked away. However, I knew in the back of my mind that, as soon as he was out of Kyle's sight, he was going to transport home.

"What do you want to talk about?" I reached the top of the porch steps.

"I wanted to apologize to you."

"Kyle, I really don't want to talk about this right now."

"Just let me finish, please."

"Okay. I am sorry for kissing you. That was wrong. Nevertheless, I just wanted you to know how I have felt for a long time."

"Kyle, don't," I told him.

"I have been waiting so long for you and Tyler to break up. And finally when I think I have a chance to tell you how I feel, you go and get with Isaac."

"Look, Kyle, I am with Isaac. We are together, and you are going to have to deal with it. I am so sorry that you feel the way you do about me. Even so, you are my best friend."

"Okay, just friends, and that's all."

Taking a step toward me, he looked me straight into my eyes. "Fine. Just tell me that kiss meant nothing to you. Tell me you didn't feel anything at all in that moment for me."

Taking in a deep breath, I looked him in his eyes as I exhaled. "It didn't mean anything, Kyle. I'm sorry." I took a step back from him and walked into the house, shutting the door behind me.

Standing there with my back on the door, I could hear Kyle walking down the stairs. I missed my best friend so much: our conversations and the things we did together. I knew none of that would ever be the same again. Walking upstairs to my room, I closed my door behind me.

Walking into my bathroom, I got changed for bed. Coming out of my bathroom, I climbed into my bed and slid under my covers. I reached over and turned off my lamp on my nightstand, laid my head on my pillow, and fell asleep.

In the middle of the night, Kyle came back over to my house. He climbed up the ladder to my room and very quietly climbed through the window. Walking over to me, he couldn't help but smile as he leaned down to kiss me on the cheek. He reached into his back pocket and took out a little box with a note attached to it. He placed it on my pillow and quietly climbed back out the window and down the ladder.

The next morning, I woke up feeling very well rested. Not realizing what was on my pillow, I stretched my arms above my head, knocking the box in the trash basket by my bed.

I got up out of bed and took a shower. Today was going to be a good day. Washing suds out of my hair and the soap off my body, I turned off the water. I grabbed my towel and wrapped it around me as I stepped out of the shower.

Walking into my room, I could hear my phone begin to ring. I walked over to my nightstand and answered it.

"Hello," I answered.

"Hey, beautiful," Isaac said on the other end of the phone. "How are you this morning? I hope you slept well."

"Of course I did. I spent the night dreaming of you."

"How can I argue with that?" he asked on the other end of the phone.

"Is everything okay?" I asked.

"Yes, of course. I just really needed to hear your voice."

"You are so sweet."

"I try to be."

"Hey, are you going to the game tonight?"

"Of course, I'm coming. You're going to be cheering. I wouldn't miss that for the world."

"Oh, really?"

"Yes, really. You know I love the way you look in that skirt."

"Whatever." I was blushing on the other end of the phone. "So what time should I be at your house for dinner?"

"You can come around five. That way, we both have enough time to get ready for the game tonight."

"Sounds like a plan."

"Do you want to ride to the game together?" he asked.

"I would love to, but I'm going to pick up Amy and Chelsea to ride to the game tonight."

"Okay, that's fine. I guess I will see you at school then."

"Yes, I will see you there."

"Okay. Bye."

"Bye."

Today at school just flew by really fast. School, to say the least, was actually fun. We had our pep rally during third period, and the marching band with the cheerleaders marched through the hallways of the school. Everyone came out of the classrooms to watch.

After school was over, I rushed home to get ready for the early dinner that my family and I were having with Isaac. Walking through the front door, I could hear my aunt and uncle in the kitchen preparing dinner.

"Hey, guys," I said, entering the kitchen.

"Hey, sweetie," they both said at the same time.

"It smells really good in here."

"We are cooking chicken parmesan with delicious garlic breadsticks," said Kristen.

"That sounds great," I said to her.

"So Isaac is coming to dinner," said Matthew in a cautious tone.

"Please be nice to him. I really care about him. Aunt Kristen, please make Uncle Matthew be on his best behavior."

"I promise to be on my finest behavior, sweetie."

"Thank you," I said to him. "I'm going to go upstairs and get washed up for dinner. Isaac will be here in about an hour."

"Okay, sweetie, everything will be ready by then."

An hour later, I heard the doorbell ring downstairs. I rushed down the stairs to the front door. Opening the door, I saw Isaac standing there, looking as handsome as ever with a beautiful bouquet of flowers.

"Hey, you," I said to him.

"Hey," he replied back. "Come in."

As the door closed behind him, my aunt and uncle were coming out of the dining room over to us. Standing beside Isaac, I decided to get the introductions out of the way.

"Isaac, this is Aunt Kristen, who you have already met, and this is Uncle Matthew."

"Mrs. Thompson, it is a pleasure to meet you again. These are for you." He handed her the bouquet of flowers.

"Thank you, Isaac, and it is a pleasure to meet you again as well."

"Hi, Mr. Thompson. It's good to finally meet you, sir. Nichole has told me nothing but great things, sir." Isaac reached out his hand for my uncle to shake it. "It's good to meet you too," Isaac said to my uncle as he shook his hand.

"Well, Isaac, Nichole is very important to us. So if you hurt her, I will hurt you."

"Uncle Matthew," I said to him in an embarrassing tone.

"I understand, sir. Duly noted."

"Why don't we all head into the dining room and I will go put these in some water?"

Taking my seat next to Isaac, I was so nervous of how dinner would go. However, strangely enough, Isaac wasn't nervous at all. Sitting at the table, everyone enjoyed the meal that was prepared. Of course, Matthew and Kristen asked him every question in the book, and he didn't pause at anything. He answered every question with so much confidence and sureness. After dinner, Isaac insisted that he wash all the dishes and put the leftovers away with me before he left. After we all said our good-byes, I headed upstairs to get ready for the game. While putting on my makeup and doing my hair for the game, I received a call from Kyle.

Picking up my phone, all I could do was look at it. *What would I say to him?*

Hitting the ignore button on my phone, I put it down and finished doing what I was doing. Finishing with my hair and makeup, I slipped into my black and orange cheer uniform, put on my socks and shoes, and headed out the door.

Picking up Amy and Chelsea for the game felt like old times. It felt like we were freshmen on our way to our first football game as cheerleaders. Only now, we were going to our first football game as seniors. *Man, how time flies by. Looking back over my high school years, I can really say I have enjoyed every bit of it. Now as a senior, I know it is only going to get better.*

Arriving at the school was very exciting. Grabbing our bags, we walked to the football field ready to cheer on our school. It really felt like old times again. Standing in formation with Samantha and me in the front, I looked into the crowd to see if I saw Isaac. There he was, sitting in the middle of the bleachers, looking handsome as ever and watching me with a smile on his face. *I am so lucky.*

Looking to my far right, I noticed Kyle sitting at the top of the bleachers. He wasn't even looking at me. He just seemed so lost. *He was so unhappy because of me.* I just wanted to walk up to him and hug him. Nevertheless, our friendship wasn't the same anymore.

Not realizing we were about to start a cheer, Samantha tapped me on the shoulder to snap me out of daydreaming.

"Are you okay?" she asked.

"Yes, I am fine. Let's just do a cheer," I said to her.

As we began to do a cheer, the crowd jumped up off their feet with joy as the football team scored a touchdown. The band began to play, and the crowd started to rock side to side to the beat. Just when things were calming down, the lights went off on the field. It was pitch-dark.

The entire place was silent. After a couple seconds, the lights came back on, and everyone heard a scream. Looking on the field, I saw a dead body that belonged to one of the referees. Everyone at the game started to run and panic. Looking around, trying to find Isaac, I felt a hand grab my arm and throw me in the middle of the field. Not sure what was going on, I tried to get up, but I couldn't move my right arm.

I lay back on the ground and started to think of Isaac, and within a second, he was right by my side. Looking up at him, I was so scared at the chaos that was taking place.

"Isaac, I can't move my arm."

"Your shoulder is dislocated." Gently grabbing my arm, he quickly snapped it back into place.

While I was screaming at the top of my lungs, he helped me up quickly to my feet. In the corner of my eye, I could see Kyle approaching me quickly.

"Nichole, are you okay?"

"Yes, I'm fine," I said while in pain.

"Kyle, listen to me. You need to take her and drive her home," said Isaac. "Don't stop for anything. Go hurry."

Not really realizing what was going on, I could hear Kyle telling me everything was going to be okay as he carried me to my car. Placing me on the passenger's side, he quickly shut the door and ran to get into the driver's seat. He started up the engine and drove away from the field.

"Where is Isaac?" I asked with a lot of concern in my voice.

"He's back at the field. He told me to take you home."

"Turn around." I demanded.

"No, he told me to take you home."

"We can't just leave him there. Turn this car around now!" I yelled.

"Fine," Kyle said to me.

While Kyle was pulling up back to the field, I jumped out the car and ran to the field where I saw Isaac. Feeling the pain shoot up my arm, I knew I had to help Isaac.

Looking onto the field, I saw him fighting two muscular men in grey suits. I started running full speed at them to help Isaac, not even caring about my shoulder. Within a second, a powerful force pulled me back, and I landed roughly on the ground. Rolling over to my back, I saw Kyle squatting down next to me.

"Nichole, get up," said Kyle.

Slowly getting up, my back was facing Isaac. "Go back to the car," I told Kyle.

"Not unless you come with me."

"Go back to the car," I said, ordering him.

As I started to tell him again, Kyle noticed one of the men throwing a knife at me.

"Nichole, watch out!" Kyle yelled at me as he pushed me to the ground.

Sitting up to face Kyle, I looked up at him and saw a knife was in his chest. Looking me in my eyes, he fell to his knees and onto his back. I sat up and looked at Kyle. Frozen in shook, I managed to look over at Isaac fighting. Slowly, I stood to my feet. With both hands balled up into fists, I felt my body heating up. My eyes burned as I began to feel my power going through my body.

Within a second, I lost control and ran full speed at the two men. I quickly reached the first man and grabbed his neck and broke it with one snap. I then jumped behind the second guy who stabbed Kyle and grabbed his arm. With every force inside of me, I broke his arm in two. Grabbing his other arm, I put my knee in his chest.

"Who sent you here?" I demanded.

"I'm not telling you anything."

Not hearing what I wanted to hear, I broke his other arm. Grabbing him by the neck, I lifted him up in the air with one arm.

"You stabbed my best friend, and since you won't tell me what I want to know, I'm going to kill you."

"Nichole, don't," said Isaac.

Before he could finish his sentence, I snapped his neck and threw him on the ground. Walking over to Kyle, I could feel myself gaining control back over my body as my eyes turned back to their natural color. Kneeling down, I placed Kyle's head carefully onto my lap.

"I'm so sorry," Kyle whispered to me.

"Save your breath. You're going to be fine," I told him. "I'm so sorry for not being there for you when you needed me to."

"No, you were."

"Just breathe." The tears continued to run down my cheeks.

"Nichole, I love you, and I have always been in love with you. I wanted you to know that."

As I lowered my chin into my chest, I began to cry even harder. Opening my eyes, I looked at Kyle and smiled.

"I love you too." I slowly bent down and kissed him on his lips.

Slowly pulling away, Kyle smiled at me. "Thank you," he whispered to me and closed his eyes to take his last breath.

"No, Kyle. Come on. Kyle, please just breathe." I pleaded for him. "Just breathe. Come on, Kyle. Please."

Closing my eyes, I held Kyle close to me as I broke down and cried for my best friend. Wanting to comfort me, Isaac walked up to me and placed his hand on my shoulder.

"We have to go," Isaac said.

"No!" I screamed at him. "Just get away from me."

"Nichole."

"Don't. Just leave me alone."

Looking at me, he knew I had lost a part of myself. And there was nothing he could do in this moment to make it better.

"I have to get him out of here." Closing my eyes, I concentrated very hard, and then within a blank of an eye, they were gone.

CHAPTER 17

Opening my eyes, I realized we were on Kyle's porch. I gently laid his head on the floor and stood to my feet. Standing there in complete shock, I got up the courage to ring the doorbell.

Ringing the doorbell, I just stood there looking at him. I couldn't let his mother see me. I ran behind the tree in front of his house. Peeking around the tree, I watched as his mother opened the door. I saw the look on her face as she noticed her son laying there breathless. His mother fell to the floor in disbelief, grabbing her son in her arms and crying out for help.

Falling to the ground behind the tree, I dug my face into my hands and cried. Not being able to take it anymore, I transported myself into my room. Running into my bathroom, I got into the shower and turned on the water. I started washing Kyle's blood off my hands, face, arms, and legs. Kneeling down in the shower, I curled up in the corner of the shower and began to really break down.

I turned off the water and stepped out of the shower to grab my towel and dry off. Putting on some clean clothes, I sat on the side of my bed by my trash can. Looking down at my floor, I glanced at my trash can and saw a box with a note taped to it. I reached down and grabbed it. Positioning myself in the middle of my bed, I read the note.

> *Dear Nichole, we have known each other for so long. Watching you grow into the beautiful person you have become has made me fall in love with you. I love you, Nichole, and it is because I love you that I am going to respect your wishes and be there for you. I can't bear the thought of losing you in my life. I am so sorry for the pain I have caused you. So I got this for you as a peace offering. I hope you like it. Love, Kyle.*

Putting the note down beside me, I wiped away tears from my face and opened the box. Inside was a necklace. Lifting the necklace from the box, I noticed it had a little silver Eiffel Tower dangling from it. Tears streamed down my face as I held the necklace in my hand.

I then heard a knock at my door. The door opened, and Aunt Kristen came in and sat on the bed with me.

"Honey, I'm so sorry. I just heard."

"I miss him, Aunt Kristen. I miss him so much." I pleaded as I fell into her arms.

My aunt comforted me all night as we both grieved over a loving friend.

Three days had passed since Kyle's death, and I was taking it very roughly. Sitting in my room for the past three days, I knew everyone was very concerned about me. I didn't really sleep, and I barely ate anything. I hadn't talked to anyone since Kyle's death: no phone calls, no face-to-face contact, and not even texting. However, I didn't care. All I wanted was my best friend back.

Knocking on my door, my uncle walked into my room. Walking over to me, he stood behind me as I looked into my mirror.

"It's time to go to the funeral, sweetie."

"I'm not going."

"Nichole, you have to go. Kyle would want you there."

Brushing my hair, I continued to stand in front of my mirror. Turning around to look at my uncle, I had the most motionless look on my face.

"No, Kyle would want to be here alive, breathing and talking. However, because of me, he can't do any of those things."

"What do you mean, sweetie?" Matthew asked.

Closing my eyes, a tear ran down my cheek. "Just forget about it, and let's just go to this funeral."

I opened my eyes. Walking out of my room, I slowly walked downstairs. Grabbing my sweater off the coat rack, I walked outside to get into the car.

Riding in the car, I sat in the backseat and looked out the window. We passed by an old playground where Kyle and I used to play as children. I could still see him chasing me and laughing at the top of his lungs. Smiling at the memory, I closed my eyes and wiped away my tears. Arriving at the church, I felt different, not like myself. I felt as if someone had ripped a part of me out of my body.

Sitting there quietly in the church, I didn't say a word or show any emotion. Aunt Kristen reached for my hand, and I moved it away from her. Not being able to take the pain anymore, I stood up and ran out of the church.

"Nichole, wait," my aunt yelled at me.

But it was too late. Running away from the church, I felt like I could finally breathe. Not even caring about the cars coming my way, I continued running. I ran full speed, taking off my sweater and shoes, and kept running.

Sitting in his living room, Isaac couldn't help but worry about me. It had been three days, and he hadn't talked to me. He thought that I wouldn't even see him. Sitting on the couch in the living room of his house, his phone began ringing on the coffee table. Reaching for it, he answered it while putting it to his ear.

"Hello," he answered.

"Isaac, hi. This is Amy. Is Nichole over there with you?"

"No, I haven't talked to her in three days. Why?"

"We haven't seen her since Kyle's funeral. She got up in the middle of the service and ran out of the church. No one has seen or heard from her since."

"Don't worry. I'm going to find her. I'll call you when she is with me."

"Okay."

"Bye."

"Bye."

Going to every place he could think of, he transported himself there. Not getting any luck, he thought very carefully. He knew he should stop thinking of all the places that he thought I would be. Where would I go to spend time with Kyle? And then it hit him.

Transporting into the school, he looked down the hallway and saw me passed out on the floor below Kyle's locker. As he got closer, he could tell I had not been there long because I was still soaked from the rain. Lifting me up into his arms, he transported me back to his house.

Laying me on the couch, Isaac took off my wet clothes, put me in one of his dress shirts, and covered me up with a blanket. During that process, I began to wake up. He could tell I was very confused as to what was going on.

"You're going to be fine."

Within that second, I was back asleep. I continued to do this for the next four hours.

Dialing Amy's number on his phone, he waited for her to answer as he walked into the foyer to talk to her.

"Hey, did you find her?" asked Amy.

"Yes, she is right here on my couch asleep."

"Call her aunt and uncle. Let them know that she is fine and say she is at your house and just needed to get away or something."

"Okay, I'll think of something."

"All right."

"Bye."

"Thanks, Isaac. You're a really good guy," said Amy.

"Thanks." Isaac took a seat on the coffee table in front of me.

"Bye."

"Bye."

Slowly waking up, I started to look around and in front of me to notice Isaac.

"Isaac," I said in a confused voice.

"Hey, how you doing?" he asked.

Slowly lifting myself up so I was sitting upright, I moved my hair from my face. "How did I get here?"

"Well, after you ran out of the church and went missing, Amy called me. I went out to look for you and found you passed out below Kyle's locker at school. I transported us both here and placed you on the couch so you could rest. You have been in and out for the past four hours."

"I should call Kristen and Matthew."

"No need. They think you are at Amy's just clearing your head."

Smiling lightly, I noticed I was wearing one of Isaac's shirts. "So how did I get into your shirt?"

"I put it on you. Don't worry. I was a gentleman."

"Thank you."

Gently touching his hand, I smiled lightly at him. "I'm sorry if I have been so distant with you. I just needed some time to myself."

"It's fine. I understand. I'm just glad you're okay."

Pulling back my hand from his, I sat back and looked in my lap. "Who sent those men?" I asked under my breath.

"Valcuse," he answered very firmly.

"They wanted to kill me, didn't they?"

"Yes, they wanted to kill you before you could learn how to use your powers properly. I guess they underestimated how powerful you really are."

"It's my fault Kyle is dead."

"No, Nichole," said Isaac as he sat next to me.

"Yes, it is. He turned the car around because of me, and he got stabbed because of me. It's all my fault." Tears began to flow down my cheeks.

Placing my hands in his, Isaac turned to face me. "Look at me." Lifting my head, I looked him in his eyes. "It is not your fault. Nevertheless, I know it's not your fault, okay?" He cut me off before

I could finish what I was saying. "Listen to me. You are an amazing person, Nichole. Kyle would not want you to blame yourself for this. It's not your fault."

Moving in closer to me, he wiped away a tear from my cheek with his thumb. Slowly lifting his other hand, he gently slid his thumb across my bottom lip. I closed my eyes as I felt the warmth of his soft thumb on my lip. He then leaned in slowly to me so the tips of our noses were touching. Grabbing his shirt, I pulled him into me for our lips to connect in a passionate kiss. *Is this really happening right now?*

He slowly pulled away and stood to his feet. He reached out his hand as an invitation to me. And like always, I accepted. Standing to my feet, he placed my cheek in his hand and kissed me gently as he transported us both to his room. Standing in front of his bed, I could feel my body tingle with desire.

Turning me around so I was facing the bed, he moved my hair to one side of my shoulder and kissed my neck very gently. I felt as though I could stand it no longer as my eyes closed in pleasure. I reached my arm up and grabbed the back of his neck to help support me on my feet. Sliding both hands in front of me, he slowly unbuttoned the shirt I was wearing. Unbuttoning the last button, he slowly slid the shirt down my shoulders, to my arms, and then to the floor. Revealing my body, he stealthily turned me around to face him.

"You are so beautiful," Isaac whispered to me on my lips.

Placing his lips on mine, he kissed me with so much passion. I felt so light on my feet. Sliding my hands from his chest down to his abs, I slowly pulled his shirt over his head. I made sure to notice every part of his body that was being revealed. I could hear his breathing go from fair to very sharp as I unbuckled his belt and unbuttoned his pants, showing the top of his briefs. I slowly pulled his pants and briefs down to his ankles.

Standing back up to my feet, I kissed him as he freed his legs out of his pants. Pulling me in closer to him, I could feel his hands exploring my body as he unhooked my bra. Sliding the straps from my arms, it fell to the floor between us.

Slowly removing my boy shorts, I could feel them sliding down my legs as they hit the ground. Stepping out of them, I wrapped my arms around his neck. He pulled me in even closer into him, making our bare bodies touch as we both felt the warmth between each other.

Lifting me up above his waist, I wrapped my legs around him, and he gently placed me in the middle of his bed. He kissed me slowly, moving from my lips to my neck, to my collarbone, to the middle of my breast, and down to my navel. He then slid his hand from my knee, up to my thigh, and up to my waist. I could feel the sensation going through my body as I arched my back. I felt his weight move back up to me. I flattened my back to the bed as he placed his lips on my neck.

Lifting himself up, he looked me in my eyes and smiled at me. "Are you okay?"

"Yes."

"You sure you want to do this?"

Placing both hands on his face, I smiled back at him. "I've never been surer of anything in my life. I love you."

"I love you too."

I pulled him in close to me for a kiss. As he slowly made our bodies become one, I gasped for air from the pain.

"Do you want me to stop?" he asked.

"No, I'm okay. Just kiss me."

The pain slowly eased away with every stroke that entered my body, and we began making love to each other for the first time. Making our bodies move as one made him fit between my thighs perfectly. The feeling that was going through my body was intoxicating. I wanted nothing more than to feel this way forever, for this could not have been a more perfect moment. I moved my hands up and down his back as if it were a maze.

Moving as one, he rolled over to his back, placing me sitting on top of him as I moved my hips in a smooth motion. Moving his hands from my thighs, he placed his right hand on my waist, and his left hand cupped my breast. As I threw my head back in passion, the feeling between our bodies began to get intense. Lifting up to me, Isaac planted a kiss in the middle of my chest. Bringing my head back to him, I lifted his chin and kissed him passionately.

Holding each other close, we both let go and let our bodies explode in the intense feeling that we both had been waiting for. Looking into Isaac's eyes, a tear fell from my right eye.

"Baby, why are you crying? Did I hurt you?"

"No, I'm fine. It's just for so long that I wanted a love that is pure and strongly desired. The kind of love that makes you look at the other person like nothing else in the world matters, and thanks to you, I finally have that. You truly are the love of my life, Isaac."

"You have always been mine, Nichole."

"I love you," I said to him.

"I love you too, always."

Lowering ourselves back to the bed, we both laid there in silence, holding each other as we drifted into a peaceful sleep. Lying on my side, I slid my hand on the bed, looking for Isaac. Opening my eyes, I noticed he was not there. Sitting up in the bed, I looked around the room to notice him standing next to the window, looking outside as it rained. Silently sliding out of the bed, I wrapped the sheet around me and walked over to him. After I kissed him on his back, he turned around to face me with a very satisfied look on his face.

"You okay?" I asked.

"Yes, I'm perfect."

"That was the most amazing and perfect experience in my life."

Pulling me in close to him, he looked me in my eyes and smiled. "I love you."

"I love you too."

While kissing each other with all the passion in our bodies, Isaac lifted me up and took me back to the bed, and we made love all over again, ending the night wrapped fast asleep in each other's arms.

CHAPTER 18

Waking up the next morning on Isaac's chest just felt so normal. *How did I ever get so lucky?* I thought to myself.

"Good morning," he said to me as he slowly opened his eyes.

"Good morning."

"You're just perfect. Do you know that?" he asked.

"Well, I wouldn't say that I'm perfect."

"Yes, you are. You know you should give yourself more credit than you do. You are a wonderful and very intelligent person." Looking down at me, he kissed me on the top of my head while my head rested on his chest.

"Thank you." I smiled. "I guess last night was that perfect moment you were talking about. I couldn't have timed it any better." Laying there indulging in the moment that we were sharing together, a thought suddenly crossed my mind. "Can I ask you a question?"

"Sure, you can ask me anything."

"Can you train me?"

Looking at me with a smile on his face, he slowly lifted my chin with his hand to plant a kiss on my lips. "I thought we were doing some training last night." He moved his hand from my chin down to the middle of my back.

"Not that kind of training," I said with a slight smirk on my face.

Looking into my eyes with confusion, he quickly understood what I meant and sat up on his side to face me at eye level. "Why do you want me to train you?"

Looking down at the bed, I exhaled a shaking breath. "You know why."

Lifting the sheets off his body, he got out of the bed and got dressed. "Nichole, I can't do that."

Putting my attention back on him, I lifted myself up on my bottom. "Why not?"

"You have no idea what you are asking me to do."

"Isaac, this isn't about you."

"Yes, it is," he said to me. "I am with you now and forever, so, yes, it is about me if it involves you." Walking over to the bed, he sat on the edge, taking my hand. "If anything happened to you, I don't know what I would do."

"Nothing is going to happen to me, okay." I moved in closer to him. "This is something I have to do. I can't just stand back and let Kyle's death mean nothing. Kyle died trying to protect me from Valcuse's men who were sent to kill me. Please help me, Isaac. Kyle is not the only reason that I want to stand up to Valcuse." I placed his cheek in my hand. "My future with you is the most important thing to me. I want to protect that. From what you tell me, a Valcuse-free life sounds pretty perfect, right?"

"Yes, it does." He smiled. "Okay, I will train you. I will teach you everything I know. Just promise me something."

"Anything," I replied.

"Promise me that I will not lose you."

"Listen to me. You are not going to lose me. I promise you that. I am yours forever. This is just something I have to do. It's my destiny, remember?"

Climbing on top of him, I made him lean back onto the bed. I started kissing him in a very seductive way. Disconnecting his lips from mine, he let out a sigh. "I thought you wanted me to train you."

I leaned in close to him, making our lips touch but not connect. "What do you think we are about to do right now? Practice makes perfect, right?"

Smiling at each other, we connected our lips in a very slow pace. Rolling me over to my back, he sat up, took off his shirt, and leaned back down to kiss me. Sliding back under the sheets with me, we began to seduce each other, secretly thinking that this could be the last time that we could hold each other.

Later that afternoon, after calling my aunt and uncle to let them know I was okay and I would be home afterward, Isaac and I went in his backyard to start our training. His backyard was so open—no trees, flowers, or even bushes. As I stood there, I could only see the green grass, the open sky, and a beautiful lake. The grass was just as soft on the bottom of your feet as if you were walking on cotton. The sky was as clear as a glass of water. The lake in the back of his home looked so peaceful as the sun danced on the tiny waves from the wind. It really felt like a little piece of heaven on earth.

"You ready?" he asked as he stood up straight next to me.

"Yes," I answered with anticipation in my voice.

"Okay, first you have to learn how to trigger your powers with your emotions. Using your emotions helps you gain control over your powers and body. I want you to lift my cell phone out of my back pocket and make it come to you."

"That's it?" I asked with sarcasm in my voice.

"Let's just start out small."

Focusing on his phone, I tried numerous times to remove it from his back pocket, but nothing was happening.

Walking behind me, he whispered in my ear, "Combine anger with passion. Think of something that makes your blood boil just by the thought of it."

"Kyle being killed," I said with a very serious tone in my voice with my eyes closed.

"Good. Now hold that thought. Now think of something that you love and cherish deeply."

A smile came on my face. "You," I whispered.

"Okay, now combine both of those thoughts together."

As I was concentrating, his phone lifted up out of his back pocket to right in front of me.

"You're doing great. Just keep combining those two things." The phone then smoothly moved to the side of me and then back to the front of me, floating. "Okay, open your eyes."

Opening my eyes to see the phone floating in front of me was amazing. "Wow, I can't believe I'm doing this."

Walking in front of me, he grabbed his phone and looked at me with very proud eyes. "Okay, let's try something a little bigger. I want you to try to lift me." Stepping back a few steps, he looked up at the sky with a smile.

"You are kidding, right?"

"No, not at all. Lift me up into the air. All you have to do is just remember what I told you, and you will be fine."

"Okay." I focused on him. Thinking of everything Valcuse had taken from me and everything I had gained since Isaac had come into my life, I felt the warmth of my body as energy began to flow through it so smoothly.

The wind blowing against my skin made me feel so light on my feet. Continuing to focus on elevating Isaac off the ground, my eyes turned as blue as the Pacific Ocean, and my crystal also began to glow.

Carefully lifting my arm in front of Isaac, I turned my hand with palm facing the sky. As my hand began to rise, Isaac began to rise as well. Lifting my hand above my head, I looked up at Isaac and was overwhelmed in excitement.

"I did it!" I yelled with enthusiasm.

Not thinking, I dropped my hand down by my side just to enjoy the moment. Isaac quickly began to fall at a quick speed out of the air. Realizing I had stopped focusing on Isaac, I regained focus quickly enough to use my hand to force Isaac into the lake.

"I'm sorry!" I yelled as he came back up for air in the water.

Swimming back to me, he climbed out of the lake and walked over to me. "It's okay. You just have to stay focused. That's all." Isaac bent down to kiss me on the cheek. "And thank you for regaining your focus in enough time to throw me into the lake."

"You're welcome." I laughed. "What should we try next?"

Smiling back at me, he leaned in for a kiss, and before our lips touched, he disappeared.

"Isaac?" I called out as I looked around.

He was nowhere in sight. I then felt a hand on my shoulder behind me. Turning around, I stood still in front of him.

"I had to get out of those wet clothes. Now you try," he said to me. "Just think of somewhere you want to be and allow yourself to be taken there in your mind. And then make it real. I think you have already perfected this though."

Standing in front of me, he watched me as I closed my eyes and a smile came across my face. Then within a second, I was gone. Within five seconds, I was back in front of him.

"Where did you go?" he asked me.

"I went to the cliff. It was amazing. I felt so free, like nothing could stop me."

Walking over to me, he wrapped his arms around me and pulled me in close to him. "And now nothing will," Isaac whispered to me.

"Can I ask you a question?" I asked.

"Sure."

"How powerful am I?"

"I said that, when you are ready, you will not need your crystal. Your power will come from inside, and you will be one with yourself."

Pulling away very playfully, I smiled at him. "Okay, let's train some more. I want to get in as much training as possible."

We trained until the sun went down. And to tell the truth, I was actually a very quick learner. I was sad when I left Isaac's house, but in truth, I really missed my aunt and uncle. I knew they were worried about me.

CHAPTER 19

Walking into the front door of my house, I looked around and noticed how silent it was.

"Hello, anybody home?"

"We're upstairs," said Aunt Kristen.

Walking upstairs, I stood in front of their room door and knocked. They invited me into their bedroom. Opening their room door, I saw them in their bed, both reading as usual.

"Can I come in?"

"Sure, honey, come on in," my aunt said.

Walking into their room, I sat on the edge of their bed and looked at them both. "I just wanted to thank the both of you for everything you two have done for me. And I know I haven't been the easiest to live with lately."

"Sweetie, it's fine," Aunt Kristen said to me.

"No, it's not. Before I guess when I found out that I was adopted, I felt like I wasn't a part of you two anymore. Nevertheless, I now realize I have always been a part of the both of you." I felt tears in my eyes. "And if it's okay with the two of you, I would rather call you Mom and Dad because that's who you are to me."

They both looked at me. They both smiled as tears of joy filled their eyes.

"I would be honored," said Aunt Kristen.

"Of course, sweetie," said Uncle Matthew.

"What makes you think you would even have to ask? Come here, baby," Kristen told me.

Crawling in the middle of both of them, they both held me close.

"From now on, we will always be honest with one another about any and everything."

"Okay," Kristen said.

As she rested her chin at the top of my head, I shook my head in agreement. "You promise?" I asked her.

Looking at each other, both Matthew and Kristen smiled at each other.

"We promise," they both answered.

We all just laid there for a few minutes. All of us were just indulging in the moment that we were finally back on track.

The next morning, I went over to Isaac's house to see him. Being away from him for so long, I had begun to ache for him. Lying on the couch with him in front of the fireplace was so quiet and peaceful. Just lying here together, enjoying each other's presence, was more than enough for the both of us. I then felt his hand slide from my waist to my chest as he noticed the necklace that Kyle gave me.

"When did you get this?"

Looking down at my necklace, I had a smile on my face. "It's from Kyle. I found it in my trash can by my nightstand in a box the night he died. He must have left it for me, and I must have accidentally knocked it into the trash."

Looking at the charm on the necklace, he looked a little confused and then realized what the charm meant. "He knew you wanted to go to Paris, didn't he?"

"Yes, he did."

"Well, I think it's beautiful," said Isaac.

"It is, isn't it?" I said.

Looking up at me, he paused before speaking. "Can I ask you a question?"

"Sure."

"Could you ever see yourself married?"

Quickly sitting up, I slid back into the corner of the couch. "Are you—"

"No." He quickly cut me off from finishing my sentence. "I'm just curious. But could you in the near future?"

Sliding back over to him, I leaned in close to him. "I could see myself accomplishing and doing anything in the future as long as you are in it."

"You really are unpredictable, you know that, right?" Isaac said to me.

"Why? Is it really that hard for you to think I wouldn't say that?"

"No, that's not what I meant. It's just that you surprise me all the time."

After I put all of my weight onto him, he fell back onto the couch with me on top of him. "How could it be a surprise to you when we both know our futures will be together?" He couldn't do anything but smile back at me.

Lowering my head into him, I slowly connected my lips to his. "How about we do some more training before I leave to go home?"

"Okay, what power should we work on?" He smiled at me, and we disappeared and reappeared in his bedroom.

"I think this is my favorite kind of training so far."

"I was thinking the same thing." Isaac slid his hand to my lower backside.

"So how much training do we need to do today? I would say until we get tired, of course."

"However, just to warn you, it takes a while before I get tired," said Isaac.

"Well, I think I can handle it."

We both smiled at each other, and we kissed in a very seductive way. Rolling me over to my back, he traced his hand from my knee into my inner thigh, knowing that this made me go crazy. As I disconnected from his lips, I arched my back as my eyes closed in pleasure.

Moving from my lips, he slowly lowered to kiss me on the side of my neck. He unbuttoned my shirt as I started to unbuckle his pants. Slowly lowering himself into me, we both held each other close as we made love to each other for the rest of the afternoon.

That night walking into my room, I thought about facing Valcuse. Not knowing when he would show up, all I knew is that I would have to be ready to fight him. I laid down on my bed and continued to think to myself as I fell asleep.

I knew I was ready, and I absolutely had to defeat him. Waking up the next morning, Isaac was the first person on my mind. I got out of bed and walked over to my mirror and looked at my necklace with my crystal on it.

Then out of nowhere, Isaac appeared behind me.

"You know I can feel when you are thinking about me. It's like we are one."

"All I have to do is think about you, and you're there," I said to him. Turning around to him, I walked over to hug him. "What are you doing here? You know Kristen and Matthew are in the next room down the hall."

"I know, but I felt you thinking about me, and here I am." He reached in for a kiss.

I backed up and covered my mouth.

"What is it?"

"I haven't brushed my teeth yet."

"Nichole, it's okay."

"No, it's not. I'll be right back." I went into my bathroom to brush my teeth.

As I came out of the bathroom from brushing my teeth, Isaac smiled at me. "Now can I have a kiss?"

"Yes." I jumped into his arms and planted a kiss onto his lips.

As I unwrapped my legs from around him, he gently lowered me to the ground and wrapped his arms around me. "Minty fresh."

"Why, thank you," I said to him. "So I couldn't help but think about Valcuse last night and how I'm destined to defeat him." I walked over to my bed and sat on the edge.

"Look, all you have to do is believe in yourself as much as I do." He sat down next to me.

"You really believe in me that much?"

"Do you truly need to ask that question?"

As I smiled at him, I suddenly got a very sharp pain in my head. I grabbed my head and fell to the floor in pain.

"Nichole, what's wrong?" Isaac knelt on the floor next to me.

"It hurts."

"Nichole, please, what's going on?"

"I can hear him. I can hear his voice. Please make it stop. Please, Isaac."

Then all of a sudden, the pain stopped. Opening my eyes, I slowly sat up on my knees as Isaac helped me sit back up against my bed.

"Baby, are you okay? Talk to me, please."

I opened my eyes and looked into his. "It was Valcuse. I could hear his voice. He told me that he wants to meet me tonight."

"Where did he want you to meet him?"

"He said in the woods where my parents were killed. My real parents. He said I would know where."

As we sat on the floor in shock, Matthew and Kristen began to knock on the door with a worried sound in their voices.

"Nichole, are you okay?"

"Yeah, I'm fine."

"Nichole, open the door, please," said Kristen.

"No, I'm okay."

"Nichole, open this door, or I will break it down on the count of three," said Matthew. "One, two."

And before he could say three, I opened the door. "See, I'm fine."

"Why were you screaming?" asked Matthew.

"I stubbed my toe on my desk."

Standing there in my doorway, they both looked at each other.

"Okay, well, be more careful walking around in there," said Kristen.

"All right. I will." I closed the door, and they walked away. "Isaac, where did you go?"

"I'm right here." He came out of my closet.

"The closet? Really? You could have disappeared or anything, and you decide to hide in a closet."

"Does it seriously matter?"

"You're right."

"So what are you going to do?" he asked me.

"I'm going to meet him tonight. I mean, I have no other choice, right?"

"Well, I'm coming with you. I'm not letting you out of my sight, no matter what you are destined to do. I will meet you back here at six, and we will head there then."

"But what if we lose this fight, Isaac?"

"Hey, don't even say that. We are going to be just fine. You assured me of that. Besides, the sooner this is over, the earlier we can get back to our lives together."

"You're right. We are both going to be fine."

He leaned down to kiss me on my forehead, and within a second, he disappeared as his lips touched my skin. I stood there. *I can't have any doubts. No matter what it takes, I will defeat Valcuse tonight.*

The rest of the day passed by very quickly for I knew that the time I had been waiting for was here as I looked at the clock. Isaac was outside my window, waiting for me to come out of the house.

Walking downstairs, I saw Matthew and Kristen cuddled up on the couch watching a movie.

"Hey, you guys. Watching a movie?" I asked.

"Yeah, you want to join us?" Kristen asked.

"No, I actually was going to stay the night at Amy's if that's okay."

"Yeah, just drive safe, all right?"

Realizing this could be my last time seeing them, I just stood there and smiled at them.

"Are you okay, sweetie?" Kristen asked.

"I'm fine. I just really love you guys a lot."

"We love you too, sweetie."

"Well, I'll see you guys later."

"Okay. Bye."

"Bye."

"Well, that was weird," said Matthew. "Should we be worried?"

"Not at all. Now let's finish this movie," said Kristen.

Closing the door behind me, I walked down the steps of my porch and walked up to Isaac.

"Are you ready?" he asked.

Taking both of his hands into mine, I looked up at him. As I wanted so much to say no, my pride wouldn't dare to allow me to say it. "As ready as I will ever be." Closing my eyes, I thought of my dream of my real parents and the surroundings I saw.

When I opened my eyes, I knew we were in the right place. "I can feel them."

"Who?" Isaac asked me.

"My parents," I answered. "I can feel their energy here. This is the spot where they were killed. How am I able to feel them here?"

"I don't know. I have never heard of anything like that before."

From out of nowhere, three men with grey suits were right in front of us. Isaac grabbed my waist and pulled me into him very protectively.

"Valcuse would like you two to come with us."

"Where?" I asked.

"To his place," the man told us.

"Why did he want us to meet him here?"

"Valcuse will answer all questions. I assure you."

"Okay, take us to him," I said.

Walking up to us, the man touched us, and within a second, we were in an extremely huge and very modern apartment. It was on the top floor of a nice, high apartment building. It had very tall glass windows with beautiful views of a city.

"Where are we?" Isaac asked.

The man backed up toward the other two men and stood still. "New York City. This is Valcuse's penthouse suite. He will be with you shortly," the guy said to us as all three of them left the room.

After a couple seconds went by, we heard a voice in a tall chair that was at the desk in front of us. The chair was facing the huge windows that overlooked the big city.

"Hello, Nichole," the voice said.

Isaac and I stood there looking at the back of the chair, and I began to look confused.

"Wait, I recognize that voice."

"What are you talking about?" Isaac asked me.

Forcing myself to say the one name that came to mind, I knew it was impossible for it to be true. "Kyle," I said in a very impracticable tone.

Then the chair turned around, and there he was, sitting in the chair.

"Kyle," I said again in disbelief.

"Yes, that's right, Nichole. It's me. Nevertheless, most people know me as Valcuse." He was smirking.

"But how?" I began to say. "Is it possible?"

Valcuse finished for me. He stood up and walked in front of the desk to stand in front of it. "Wait, before I tell you, I have to ask: Are you surprised?" he asked sarcastically.

As I stood there, I continued to look in disbelief.

"Well, from the look you are giving me right now, I would say yes."

Shaking my head in disbelief, I fought back the tears that were forming in my eyes. "No. No, this is not possible. You're dead."

All of a sudden, he pushed off the desk, appeared in front of me, and threw Isaac up against the wall with his powers. Isaac watched Valcuse's every move, unable to move from the wall because of Valcuse's powers holding him in place. He placed his hand gently on my face as I looked into his eyes with tears in mine.

"Don't touch her!" Isaac yelled with rage in his voice.

"You're dead. You died in my arms," I said to him with sadness in my voice.

"I am standing right here in front of you. How can I be dead?"

"Nichole, that's not Kyle. He has been tricking you this whole time."

Valcuse turned his head to look at Isaac and stood up straight. "I never liked you."

Valcuse then lifted up his hand and threw Isaac out of the room through the double doors.

I turned around with a very worried look in my eyes. He then closed the doors shut with a wave of his hand and looked back at me. Isaac stood to his feet and tried to bust into the room. I turned back around to face Valcuse.

"Let Isaac go." I demanded. "He has nothing to do with this."

"However, you see he has everything to do with this." He began to walk in circles around me. "He is the reason you now know everything about this new life you have and even what you are destined for."

"So what! Just let him go. You and I can settle this," I said to him.

"Now, you know I can't do that. Besides, we both know that he is not going to leave your side anyway. So I have to kill him. And if I kill him, I might even consider letting you live. Well, that is if you will be with me. And I am pretty sure you will do it because then you won't have anybody else but me."

Backing up away from Valcuse, I lifted my head up with pride. "You see, that's where you are wrong. I have a family, and I also know that you can't kill me."

Looking worried that I knew something I wasn't supposed to know, he stopped walking in circles, stood in front of me, and looked me in the eyes. "You want to know how I know that. Please inform me," he said.

"Because if you could kill me, I would be dead right now. I am too powerful for you."

Valcuse became very angry at my answer, knowing it was the truth deep inside. Raising his hand, he slapped me to the other side of the room into a bookshelf, and I fell to the floor.

Slowly getting up, I looked up at Valcuse and smiled. "What's the matter? Can't handle the truth?"

"Do not make me kill you," he said to me.

"Do it," I told him.

With rage building inside of him, he lifted his hand and threw me into the desk. I fell up against the wall. Getting up, I stood still up against the wall. As my eyes turned blue, my crystal began to glow brighter than ever before. Looking in disbelief, Valcuse stood still with fear.

"That's not possible. That crystal was destroyed when I killed your parents. I made sure you and your crystal could never become one."

"You killed my parents." Throwing the desk out of the way, I charged after Valcuse with full force.

He lifted up his hand again and threw me through the double doors, making me slide on the floor.

Isaac ran over to me and helped me up. "Are you okay?"

"Yes, I'm fine."

"Are you okay?"

"Yes."

"Why, isn't this sweet?" said Valcuse. "Well, if you want to be together so badly, I guess you two can die together."

Five men appeared out of nowhere, surrounding us.

"Kill them." Valcuse ordered.

We moved in close to each other with our backs together.

"Remember what I told you, anger and passion," Isaac whispered to me.

As I stood there listening to him, my eyes turned blue as I concentrated on what he just whispered to me. Isaac ran toward two men in grey suits who were in front of him and grabbed one by the neck and broke it. He then lifted up his hand and threw the second guy out of the window.

Isaac turned back to look at me, and he was amazed at what he saw. Three men ran run toward me full force. Lifting up one of my hands, I made them lift up off the ground. As they dangled in the air, I balled up my fist, causing them to yell out in pain at the top of their lungs as every bone in their bodies were breaking with the tightening of my fist.

I then opened my hand, showing my palm very quickly and making their bodies explode in midair. Lowering my hand, I turned around and walked to Isaac. Pulling him by the arm gently, I looked into his eyes and kissed him.

Pulling away, I smiled at him. "This is my fight. Stay here."

"No, you're not going in that room alone," Isaac said.

I looked at Valcuse, who was watching this whole time, and then looked back at Isaac. "It's okay. Trust me." Looking back at me with worry in his eyes, he closed his eyes and let me go.

Walking into the room with Valcuse, I looked him right into his eyes with a very destructive look.

"I don't want to hurt you," he told me.

Standing in front of him a few feet away, I continued to stare. "You want to know why you can't kill me, Valcuse. Because you are in love with me. That was your biggest mistake. You care too much about me."

"You see, that's where you're wrong," he said. "When I found out about you, I decided I was going to do everything in my power to keep you from being born. So I killed the two people who were going to be your parents to stop them from getting pregnant with you so I could collect all the crystals. I thought I had destroyed your crystal just to be safe. Even so, when I killed them, little did I know, you had already been born. So I searched for you, and when I found you, I was going to kill you. However, I thought to myself, 'Why kill her when I can just keep her from finding out everything?'

"So I found a spell that could turn me into a child, and I made sure that you would never find out. That is, until Isaac showed up. Nevertheless, trust me. I am going to kill him. And when I do, I will make sure to kill him nice and slow."

"I am going to kill you," I said through my teeth.

"Give it your best shot."

Running toward each other, we both jumped into the air at each other. But at the last minute just before we reached each other, I disappeared and reappeared behind him. I grabbed his jacket and pulled him to the ground. Disappearing again, I grabbed a knife off the wall and reappeared on top of him. I ripped off his necklace and stabbed him in the heart. Slowly standing to my feet, I stepped to the side of him and knelt to his side.

"So we meet here again," Valcuse said to me.

"Yes, but this is the last time," I said to him.

He lifted up his hand and reached for my face. I grabbed his hand and placed it on my cheek.

"I always did truly love you," he said to me.

His eyes closed as his hand fell to the ground. Taking his last breath, he died and faded away in my arms forever. I stood to my feet with the crystal in one hand and the knife in the other.

Isaac walked up to me and stood at my side. "Are you going to be okay?"

"I will be."

"Let's go," he said to me.

Holding each other close, we were grateful that we both survived as we smiled and disappeared.

CHAPTER 20

Waking up the next morning, I felt so happy and relaxed. As I sat up in my bed, Isaac was sitting at my desk, looking at me.

"How long have you been sitting there?"

"Just for a couple hours. You looked so peaceful sleeping that I didn't want to wake you."

"Come here." I patted on my bed for him to sit down.

As he sat down on my bed, I noticed he had a box in his hand.

"What is that?" I asked with a curious look on my face.

"Here, open it." He handed me the box.

As I opened the box, a smile appeared on my face. Lifting the item out of the box, I noticed it was a charm bracelet. It had the charm Valcuse gave me and the crystal from around Valcuse's neck.

"I just thought that, even though the first charm came from a completely evil jerk, he was still your friend. I also thought to put the crystal that holds the power of the people who are no longer with us from our planet on there also. I couldn't think of a safer place. Now I know the first two charms are sad memories. However, they both have important meanings." He put the bracelet around my wrist. "And if you want, you can always add more to the bracelet to fill it out."

"It's beautiful. Thank you."

"You're welcome."

Standing up to his feet, he held out his hand for me. Reaching out for his hand, I stood to my feet in front of him.

"I have one more surprise for you."

I gave him a curious look.

"Close your eyes." He wrapped his arms around me and pulled me in close to him.

I could hear his heart beating steady as we stood still. Then his heartbeat became a little faster than usual. I could feel a wind on my face and the heat from the sun on my skin.

"Okay, open your eyes," he said to me.

As I opened my eyes, I was just amazed. I stood in front of two glass double doors that opened up to a balcony that looked over a beautiful city.

"Are we where I think we are?" I asked.

"Yes," he replied.

"We are in Paris," I said to myself.

The Eiffel Tower was as beautiful as I imagined it. And now it was right outside the double doors in this beautiful hotel room.

"See, I told you. Never say never," he whispered in my ear behind me.

I turned to face him. Letting a tear fall on my cheek, I smiled at Isaac as I looked up at him. "Thank you so much."

He wiped away my tear from my cheek with his thumb and smiled back at me. "Anytime."

"No, really. You have brought so much joy into my life. You make me want to be a better person. I love you."

"I love you too," he replied as we stood there in each other's arms.

"So I guess this means now that we both are going to find the rest of the remaining twelve."

"Yes, it does."

"What will happen when we find them?"

"You will lead them. Give them hope."

"With you by my side, I can do anything."

"So are you up for an adventure after you graduate high school?"

"I was born ready. Plus, there are a lot of things I want to know about my parents."

"Well, I promise you that I will help you in any way that I can."

"Actually, you could help me relieve some stress right now," I said to him in a very flirtatious tone. Pulling me into him, he kissed my lips and carried me to the bed.

Looking into his eyes, I couldn't do anything but smile, for nothing could destroy this moment. The person we had once feared was no longer a threat. And what we fought so hard to get, we now had, which was each other.

ABOUT THE AUTHOR

Addie Anthony, currently a student majoring in the Criminal Justice System and a stay at home mom. She and her husband, have three children and live in Florida. Her aspiration are in singing and acting. This is her first book